A Song in My Heart

Constance Robinson

*Promise
Romances*™

Thomas Nelson Publishers • Nashville • Camden • New York

I will sing to the Lord
as long as I live.
I will sing praise to my God while I
have my being.

Psalm 104:33

For Key, who sings the song.

Published in Nashville, Tennessee, by Thomas Nelson, Inc. and distributed in Canada by Lawson Falle, Ltd., Cambridge, Ontario.

Printed in the United States of America.

Adventures in Living Free is based on the program Adventures in Christian Living, 3117 North 7th Street, West Monroe, Louisiana, 71291. Reference to the program is used by permission.

Scripture quotations are from THE NEW KING JAMES VERSION of the Bible. Copyright © 1979, 1980, 1982, Thomas Nelson, Inc., Publishers.

ISBN 0-8407-7370-6

A figure appeared on the road before him, running.

Where had it—she—come from?

Gripping the wheel of his Cougar, Mark London searched frantically with his foot for the brake pedal. His brain blasted messages of action to his hands, his feet. But he couldn't react. Everything moved in slow motion, alcohol diluting his senses. Sheila screamed, then huddled down, burrowing her head into the seat beside him. During those seconds of frozen immobility Mark's head thundered and buzzed, his heart throbbed. Then came the dull *thud-bump* of the racing body catapulting off the car.

Would he ever forget the look on the young woman's face? Shock, mingled with fear, then instant horror? No. It would haunt him forever.

Another *thud* penetrated his brain as the woman's body bounced from the hood, sliding in the dirt and gravel beside the road.

The high-pitched squealing in his ears ceased. The car stopped. Mark realized he had locked down the brakes from the moment his dulled brain had registered the need. But that split second of delay meant his instinctive reaction came too late.

Slowly Mark uncurled his fingers from the steering wheel. They felt stiff, almost paralyzed. He opened the door and stumbled back down the road. He knew it was over. He had snuffed out a life, killed another human being. Why, why was *he* still alive? How he wished he didn't have to return along this road to see...

A dark-haired young man stood beside the body, looking down, a broken liquor bottle in his hand. "You did this?"

Mute, Mark nodded his head. It couldn't have been long, Mark knew, that they stood there staring at the bruised, ravaged form of a once lovely woman. And yet, in those few seconds his whole life changed.

What ifs rebounded in his brain. If he hadn't been drinking. If he hadn't been driving too fast. If he had something worthwhile to do—some responsibility in his eighteen years instead of too much time and money. It came to Mark London as he gazed at the lifeless form that now he had something to do—commit his whole lifetime to pay for this one soul.

Then came voices, lights, and shouting from a house back off the road. "Roberta, Roberta, *mi hermosa*!" A boy came running ahead of the others. Sobbing in anguish, he was on his knees trying to hold the dead woman to his breast. "Carlos, *hombre malisimo*. Sister, sister, I will take care of you. Don't be afraid."

A slurred shout cut through the darkness, "Hey, Carl! What's all the noise? Hey, did you catch her? She was running scared!"

A party group came up, laughing, shouting, drinking, and scuffling playfully. The young women giggled as they approached. Carl, quiet and subdued, stood there as if fascinated by the body, then pointed at Mark. "You! Murderer! You killed her! My wife!"

Chapter One

O Sun, I look up to you,
You hang so peacefully in the sky.
So faithful, you're tried and true.
You're always shining down to bring us life.
With your light you daily show us the way,
Your beams warm against our skin.
And though you disappear and take the light of
    day,
It's, oh, so sure that you will rise again.

Lisa Beall's clear, beautiful voice filled the summer air, accented by the joyous barking of two golden collies she was walking for her grandmother. Lisa was glad she had come to Three Rocks, New Mexico, glad to be living with her darling old-fashioned grandmother—for a while.

When Lisa's mother informed her father that something had to be done about his mother living alone way out on that ranch, Lisa had impulsively volunteered to move in with Jewel Beall for the summer. After four hectic years of college—could it only be two weeks since graduation—the idea of staying near a small New Mexico town sounded restful and appealing. She needed the wide-open spaces, blessed peace and quiet, and time to think about her future.

Did she or didn't she want to try for the big time? She was lead singer for a musical group, but was that really what she wanted from life? Right now the decision was too much for her. When she asked for one summer, the members of the group, The Wind, agreed. They all needed a rest.

"O Sun, I look up to you, You hang so peacefully there." Lisa repeated the phrase trying to decide how the next verse should go. That was the joy and agony of having a tune drumming in her head; she couldn't relax until she'd written it all out.

She sang it again. A mockingbird joined her, and a scissor-tail perched on the low branch of a mesquite tree, head tilted. Cocking her head in return, dimples punctuating her wide smile, Lisa moved nimbly through the mesquite and Chinese elm trees that bordered the dry creek bed.

Through light and shadow, Lisa was pulled along in bursts of speed by the gilded collies. She resembled a shaft of sunlight herself in her sleeveless yellow jumpsuit. Her shoulder-length ash blonde hair glistened with highlights from the sun.

Barking in excitement, the two dogs, Honey and Goldie, leaped for a pile of brush and weeds. A startled roadrunner, long tail upright, dashed into the open. Frantically Lisa tried to restrain the dogs, but Goldie, the larger and younger of the two, jerked free. The chase was on! Goldie took off through the trees, his tongue hanging out. His leash dragged the ground, making dirt puffs in the air.

She could never catch Goldie and hang on to Honey at the same time. Quickly Lisa tied Honey to a gnarled mesquite root and followed Goldie's trail.

Dodging the thorny mesquites and yellow-flowering stickerweed, and running to catch the dog, Lisa didn't hear the thrumming sound of an approaching car. Goldie dashed across the pavement, under a barbed wire fence, and into another pasture with Lisa in pursuit.

The squealing brakes and the blare of a car horn brought Lisa to a sudden halt on the roadway. The sharp noises assaulted her ears as she watched Goldie gallop gayly across the field and out of sight.

Lisa whirled to face the tall man striding toward her from the car. Her mouth opened, but she never spoke a word. He seized her shoulders and lifted her up and off her feet, shaking her until her bones rattled. Lisa clamped her mouth shut to keep from biting her tongue.

"Watch where you're going, you crazy little idiot!" he shouted in her face. "You could have been killed!"

When he finally put her down, Lisa was weak and trembling, and a little in sympathy with the man. She had been careless to start across the road without looking. But he needn't storm at her so, shaking her until she felt like melting Jell-o.

Tilting her chin to insist on being set free, Lisa caught a glimpse of his chalk-white face and started to apologize. But before she could speak he crushed her to him, burying her head in his shoulder and holding her so tightly she could barely breathe. "Thank God," he was saying, "Oh, thank you, God."

He was trembling as if overcome with a chill. She had really frightened the man! Lisa forgot anger. She only wanted to comfort him, reassure him that she was all right, that everything was all right.

As she would have soothed a child, Lisa patted his broad back with her one free hand, the other still imprisoned between their bodies. She realized she ought

9

to be struggling more, but his arms held her securely. It was obvious that his intentions were honorable. He only needed a moment to recover from his shock. Besides, she was so weak from the shaking and fright that his support was welcome.

When his tremor passed Lisa hastily pushed back and faced him.

"Hey!" He exclaimed. "You're okay?"

"I was, but you shook me until my liver did handstands!" Lisa exerted more pressure against his chest, registering business suit, tie, and clean, square jawline. "Will you please let me go! I'm fine."

"I see that. Perfectly fine." His hazel eyes slowly assessed her face. "And an imbecile to run out into the road!"

"I'm not an imbecile." Her dimples disappeared. "And I'm tired of you saying so!" Until now her efforts at freedom had been conciliatory, but she'd had enough. "Let me go!"

"What's this? The 'unhand me, you villain,' act?" He laughed but didn't relinquish his hold. Those hazel eyes, sparkling brownish-green, and the beginning of a lopsided grin almost made Lisa return his smile.

"That's exactly right. Unhand me!"

He laughed again as he released her.

She stepped back, straightened her jumpsuit, and rubbed circulation into the arm which had been pinioned between them. When deprived of the warmth of his body embracing hers, she felt cold.

"I had almost caught Goldie when you came roaring around that curve, honking your horn and screeching your brakes. I hope that silly dog knows his way home."

"I wasn't roaring around that curve." His voice was cold and decisive.

Lisa didn't notice the sudden quiet emphasis. "Of course you were!"

"I never roar." His words were slow, measured, as he thrust his hands in his pockets.

"I would have heard the car if you hadn't been driving too fast."

"I wasn't driving too fast." His jawline tightened; a muscle twitched in his cheek. He took a breath. "No doubt you had your mind on something else."

"Oh, men!" Lisa laughed, tossing her hair. "You wouldn't admit it if you were in the wrong."

"I was not driving too fast!" His hands came from his pockets as if to grip her again. His eyes turned hard.

Instinctively Lisa retreated. Still she added, "Who do you think you are to be so positive—the King of Siam?" Then, because he looked ready to pounce, she withdrew another step. "I'd better be off." Turning, she ran back the way she had come.

He called after her. "Yes, get off!"

At his taunt she stopped. From this safer distance she felt courageous enough to retort. "Know-it-all man!"

His whole expression changed, his face lighting up as he laughed at her. "Do you know where you are? Or even, for that matter, where you're going?"

"Of course I do!" Shouting across the barren space she felt like a child hurling insults at another.

"Then you're not only careless, you're trespassing!" He laughed again, his eyes changing colors as they slowly inventoried her appearance.

Under this provocative attack Lisa's face became hot and flushed. Pivoting, she ran. Red from exertion and embarrassment, Lisa paused when she came near the tree where Honey was tied and held her hand to her glowing face. *Know-it-all man.* She wondered where *he* was going. Thirty, she decided. A businessman because of the light beige vested suit. Married or single? Her speculation had gone too far. Of course she didn't care a fig about his marital status.

Pushing down friendly paws, she untied the dog. "Come, Honey." The collie eagerly pulled her back down the trail to home. As they slowed to a more sedate pace, Lisa recalled the man's last taunt. "Do you know where you are? Where you're going?" Perhaps because the questions fit her uncertainty about the future, they nagged her. Trying to throw off her pensive mood Lisa again repeated the lines of the song she was writing.

O Sun, I look up to you,
You hang so peacefully in the sky.
So faithful—you're tried and true.
Shining down—

Now that phrase, was it necessary? Soon she had forgotten the unsettling incident and was joyfully singing again.

Eventually the hot desert sun made her pause beneath a large cottonwood. She finished the last portion of that verse in the shade, while a desert breeze blew the damp tendrils of hair off her face.

"What a gorgeous voice! And a lovely song!" exclaimed a young woman coming down a worn path through the mesquites toward Lisa.

"I'm still working on it. It's not finished." Lisa studied the newcomer. Today seemed her day for meeting people.

"I heard you singing and had to meet you. You're writing it? You must have talent galore! I'm Kimberly London—Kim—from over there." She made a vague gesture over her shoulder. "I was on my way to visit

Mrs. Beall because I heard her granddaughter has come to live with her. Are you?"

"Yes, I am." Lisa returned the smile of the cotton-blonde girl. "Lisa Beall."

"Then of course you have to sing at my wedding—I'm also on my way to tell your grandmother I'm engaged!" She fell into step beside Lisa and Honey.

Lisa smiled inwardly at Kim's enthusiasm and effervescent glow.

"The wedding will be in August, Lisa. You'll be here, and sing for me, won't you?" Impetuously Kim caught Lisa's arm. "Please?"

"Well…" Overwhelmed by Kim's generous, yet demanding, offer of friendship, Lisa hesitated to commit herself.

"Of course you will. I know we're going to be the best of friends!" Kim didn't allow for rejection, and Lisa accepted the dictum. Who could refuse such sincere friendliness?

"I've always wanted someone my age to live nearby," Kim bounced along and chatted. "And now I have my wish. Mrs. Beall's granddaughter. I don't get lonely because I love it out here, don't you? But it is going to be nice to have someone to share it with."

"It is beautiful," conceded Lisa, surprising herself. She was suddenly more aware of her surroundings and happier each moment since Kim had come along. "A different sort of beauty—courageous, perhaps," she mused, trying to put her vague thoughts into words. "And you can see so far!" She waved her hand to encompass the cactus, the mesquite, and the flat horizon.

"Exactly!" Kim nodded her head vigorously. "Buildings and mountains make me feel fenced in, claustrophobic. Most people don't understand at all. Mother thinks she's at the end of the earth out here. But Mark, my brother, understands. He feels just like I do, if not more so. There's nothing he likes better than riding off to the far end of the ranch and camping out alone. Just him, the sand dunes, cacti, and coyotes." Kim laughed.

"That's a little too primitive for me." Lisa tried to imagine herself camping out alone. She wasn't ready for that.

Kim had become thoughtful. "I think I understand his need to be alone and meditate. He's had a hard—" Abruptly she stopped and glanced at Lisa. "But I've been chattering like a magpie and here we are." Kim opened the back gate of the picket fence, leaving Lisa to wonder about brother Mark.

They entered Jewel Beall's large yard. It was filled with old-fashioned flowers—untrimmed and luxuriant lilac, forsythia, cannas, hollyhocks, rosebushes of every variety, morning-glory vines trailing on the fence, and bachelor buttons. Mexican clay bells, symbols of the ranch's name, hung from some of the trees.

Nearby, a kitchen garden was already planted with beans, tomatoes, cucumbers, carrots, squash, okra, black-eyed peas, and spring lettuce.

The young women strolled up the native rock path past the garden and beneath peach, apple and pecan trees. Lisa stopped at the greenhouse containing tables, planting pots, and hanging baskets of more exotic plants and flowers. A desk, typewriter, guitar and auto-harp were also in the greenhouse, for it had been designated Lisa's creative retreat.

"Every flower nods with welcome," said Kim. "It's good to be back!"

"I assume you've just returned from college as well?"

Answering with a nod, Kim fingered the leaf of an avocado tree. "I know Jewel is delighted you've come." She moved on to a blooming geranium. "She's not able to take care of all these, but she loves them too much to give them up."

"She's fun, you know." Lisa voiced a recent discovery.

"She's beautiful outside and in." Kim spoke deliberately and held Lisa's eyes as if making a point. "She insists I report regularly. She listens. She cares about me, us. Mark and I...we needed that. Not that Mother didn't try, but she was so wrapped up in her own problems that she didn't know how."

Lisa liked Kim, with her bubbling spirits and gamin smile, but she couldn't stop a twinge of jealousy. Kim knew her grandmother better than she did. But Lisa knew it was entirely her own fault.

"Do you come here often then?"

"Almost every day when I'm in town." Kim stopped moving through the plants to face Lisa again. "It's not even a mile over from our place. We've always come since school days when Mark was in junior high and I was a first grader. There was no one at our house in the afternoons, you know. We would have a snack and Grandmother Beall would hear all about our day. When Mark grew older he thought he was too big until—" Again there was an intriguing pause, and a sudden closed, sad look crossed Kim's features. "Well, anyway, Jewel is the only one who always understands."

"That explains the path through the pasture." Lisa wondered what Kim had started to say about her brother Mark. What was the mystery?

"Yes, a well-beaten path." Her eyes were nostalgic as she opened the back screen door and called, "Jewel, it's Lisa and Kim. We're coming in."

"Come in, come in!" responded a cheerful voice.

With Kim leading the way, they entered the spotless kitchen. Jewel Beall, her penetrating brown eyes like Lisa's, shook her hands free of dishwater suds. She dried

15

them on an apron as red as the brilliant poppies bordering the ceiling and decorating the white curtains. With an unconscious motion Jewel pushed a wave deeper into her silver grey hair, then extended both hands.

"Kim, dear, you're home!" They hugged ecstatically. Then holding Kim at arm's length, Jewel asked, "How are you? I see you've met my granddaughter, Lisa."

"I heard an angel singing and, as usual, plunged right in," confessed Kim with an impish smile. "And," taking a deep breath, she added, "I'm bursting with news!"

"Tell, tell."

"I'm engaged." When it came to the point, sudden solemnity overtook Kim, and she shyly, yet defiantly, thrust out her left hand exhibiting a small diamond on a simple gold band.

As Jewel exclaimed over its beauty, Lisa realized Kim was very anxious about her grandmother's reaction to this announcement. Tenderly Jewel held the hand up, tilting it this way and that so the diamond twinkled in the light.

"I like it. I like it very much, Kim." Her wise brown eyes studied Kim's. "Does it tell me what I hope it does about the lucky man?"

"I don't know, but I think so." Kim gently tugged her hand free, then nervously twisted the ring.

"Let's sit down, and you tell us all about him. Some iced tea while we visit?" As Kim pulled out a chair, Jewel took down three glasses from the cupboard.

"I'll finish," Lisa said. "You sit down."

"It's no trouble," the older woman protested as a matter of course, hanging onto the last threads of independence.

"I know, but when you do everything I feel absolutely unnecessary. Now is that fair? I want to feel needed, too."

16

"Oh, all right." Jewel relented with a fond smile. "You're too much like your father, getting your way. And I love you dearly." She took a chair and smiled at Kim. "I'm seated, so begin from the beginning. Name, age, occupation?"

"Randal Moore." Kim's eyes began to glow. "He's twenty-five, buying a farm, and does crop dusting to pay for it. And, he's wonderful!"

"Crop dusting! Airplanes! Oh, Kim!" The horror in Jewel's voice almost made Lisa drop the tea glasses she was placing on the table.

"I know." The light in her eyes dulled for just a moment. "It's dreadfully dangerous! I hope it won't last long. He tells me unless you inherit land it's very difficult to come out ahead farming. Then there are the improvements, the tractors, the water systems, and all sorts of things I don't know about. But, I'll learn."

"How does he know he wants to farm? I mean, if he hasn't done it?"

"But he has farmed." Kim answered proudly. "His uncle farms and Randal has worked with him. He earned his degree at Texas A and M."

"Where did you meet?" Jewel was determined to know all. Lisa sipped her tea and listened intently.

Kim's delighted laugh met this question. "That's the best part, which will win my case." She sustained the suspense by squeezing lemon into her tea before she laid a hand over Jewel's.

"We met at a church in Lubbock. They have a supper for the college students on Sunday nights. Randal says he stayed for the supper because he saw I was staying." A becoming flush tinted her cheeks. "We talked, and he asked me to go eat with him the next day. We played tennis. Then it was Wednesday and he had to get back to his farm. But he managed to get away every weekend

17

and come to Tech and—" She waved her hand expressively.

"So you're engaged!" Jewel nodded her head thoughtfully. "And he's a Christian?"

"Yes," Kim said as she patted the older woman's veined hand. "He is."

"Good." Jewel's face showed complete satisfaction before a concerned frown darkened her fading brown eyes. "And your mother?"

"She's of two minds. She's disappointed that he's not rich." Kim tossed her light blonde curls. "But she's enjoying planning all sorts of nuptial events."

"When do I meet this paragon?" Slyly Jewel winked at Lisa. "Does he have a friend he can bring for Lisa?"

"Probably, but I want her to meet Mark." Kim looked slightly puzzled. "You should know that. They'd be perfect for each other. And Mark needs—"

"I don't know about Mark. I'm not at all sure they would get along. You know how he's used to giving orders and having everyone jump to! Then there are his juveniles." She raised her eyebrows in emphasis.

"Jewel!" Surprised at her words, Kim set down her tea glass, sloshing the ice. "Jewel, you know he—"

"Well, we'll see. It's not for us to be matchmakers now, is it?" Jewel's admonition was gentle and accompanied with a smile.

"I should think not!" Piqued, Lisa stood and put her hands on her hips. "You talk as if I couldn't handle my own love life."

'Ohhh," breathed Kim. "Of course, you're right. You're both right. I hadn't thought." Lisa missed the understanding twinkle in Kim's eye as she glanced at Jewel.

Standing and catching Lisa's hand, Kim added, "I still want you to meet my brother Mark. Just, you know, because he's my brother. After all, you're going to sing at my wedding."

"Of course," Lisa agreed politely even while wondering about this Mark who caused Kim's sudden silences and had Jewel's adoration.

"Mark was supposed to get in today from Santa Fe because his Adventures class begins tonight."

"Today?" A connection dawned in Lisa's mind.

Kim didn't attach any importance to her question. "And he'll *have* to eat lunch tomorrow. Perhaps we can get together then." At the back door she turned. "I'll talk to him and call you later. Okay?"

Lisa watched Kim skip down the back path, like a friendly puppy. It would be nice to meet people her own age. But what sort of man was this Mark? Somehow Lisa was afraid he was a tall, dark-haired man with impossible hazel-green eyes. A know-it-all man.

Chapter Two

Mark London drove slowly down the paved state road that cut through his ranch. He crossed the cattle guard and turned onto the winding gravel road leading to his childhood home. Because his mother had thought the original homestead was too far from town, this typical southern-style edifice was built for her, with white pillars, curving drive, circular staircase, the works. She now called this mansion the Homestead.

Since he had to leave again after supper, Mark parked his Monte Carlo behind a Corvette in the front drive. *Now who could afford that kind of car*, he wondered, picking up his mail in the hall. A smudged, dirty envelope caught his eye but he stuffed it in his pocket for later.

Long strides took him quickly to the back of the center hall and out to the patio where his mother supervised a young Mexican girl setting out a tray of iced tea, tiny sandwiches, and fancy hors d'oeuvres.

"Mark! It's time you were home." After a delicate kiss on his cheek, she complained in a familiar refrain, "You never have enough time for me, leaving me way out here in the middle of nowhere, isolated. It looks like you could remember me."

"Iced tea. How nice." Mark returned her gentle hug, knowing she loved him even though she had difficulty expressing herself. "I'm here for supper, Mother, before going off again."

"Please call me Edwina, dear. You know *mother* makes me feel so old." Dismissing the maid with a wave of her hand, she sat in a fanback wicker chair. "Where do you go this evening?"

"My Adventures class, in the basement of the courthouse." Mark put two small sandwiches in his mouth and followed them with a long drink of tea. "That tastes good. I don't believe I ate lunch, now I think of it. Where's Kim? And how's Inez?"

Sighing, his mother fluttered a hand. "Your sister was here a minute ago. And Inez—well, her nephew Phil is here. He had to speak to her privately. He's probably in trouble. Of course, she has spoiled him horribly, while I..." Recalling that Mark was her audience and knew her well, she took off on another tack. "I still can't understand how your father—ah, here are Cousin Inez and Phillip now."

Inez was about Edwina's age but had neither the time nor the money to spend on self-preservation so she looked ten years older. Phillip was short, a little overweight, and still fighting pimples.

"Tea is just served, Inez." She gestured to the bountiful table, priding herself on her hospitality. "Have some. And I'm sure Phillip could do with some food. You've met Mark, haven't you, Phil?"

"I don't have time to stay. Busy tonight!" Rudely Phil ignored her. To Mark he said, "You were in Santa Fe at the legislature when I was here during Christmas break to visit Aunt Inez. I'm through with school now, so I'll be around more."

"I'm sure Inez is glad to have you. Where have they put you?"

Phil thrust out his chest. "I'm on my own, answering to no one," he emphasized gruffly. "I have an apartment in town. I'm going." This last was directed at Inez.

"That's your car then, the Corvette?" pursued Mark.

"A beaut, isn't it!" Phil couldn't resist the chance to brag. "Graduation present from the estate of the old man." Then he grumbled, "No faith in me. But I'll show 'em. I'm going into big business—and soon." He frowned. "Don't forget what I said, Aunt. I've got to have it or else!" On that note he grabbed a handful of sandwiches and loped through the hall and out the front door.

"Some problem, Inez?" Mark filled a plate for her.

Inez, Phil's guardian since the recent death of his parents, looked tired as she put a hand on the wicker chair for support and sat down heavily. "Only money. He needs money."

Edwina laughed sharply. "Who doesn't need money? With the allowance Mark keeps me on, I can't even play Bridge tonight!" But knowing Mark disapproved of her playing for money she switched to another tribulation. "With my darling Kimberly announcing her engagement and all the parties that requires, I don't see how I'll manage."

"Mother—Edwina." Mark corrected himself, trying to soothe her ruffled feathers. "You know I'll gladly finance all the necessary pageantry for Kim. If you need money just ask. Have I ever refused you?"

"That's not the point." Her eyes took on a lost, far-away look. It was the look they'd had for so long after her parents had died. "To think, that I—your own mother—must ask for money. Not to mention your leaving me all alone here in this wasteland, with no neighbors."

"You're forgetting Mrs. Beall and Inez."

"Sweet Inez," agreed Edwina. Inez, still lost in her problems, didn't notice her condescending smile. "Such a good idea I had when Kim decided to go off to school. I would have gone mad in this desolate hole without you. Our little games of Canasta have kept me from being bored to tears." After the compliment, as much for herself as for Inez, her tone became tepid. "Jewel Beall. What sort of neighbor is she? She never even plays Bridge. Besides, she's old."

Inez pulled herself from her problems. "I understand a granddaughter just out of college has come to live with her."

"I can't imagine her staying in a dead place like this for long." Edwina relished every opportunity to remind all that she had grown up a wealthy city girl. "Why, there aren't even any eligible men—except you, Mark." She narrowed her eyes in thought.

"Me! What on earth—"

"Of course you, Mark. You're the most eligible bachelor around. Which reminds me, Sheila Richardson-Baird called this morning. She's so young to be a widow. The Richardsons are important people."

"I don't have time," objected Mark, an instinctive vision of horror forever associated in his mind with Sheila.

"You always say that. Time, time!" Edwina stirred the lemon in her tea. "It's those juvenile delinquents. If you would forget about trying to help them, you'd have time to think about yourself some."

"I am thinking about myself. I was like them once," reminded Mark in a level, not-to-be-ignored tone. "I needed help. You know—" Ever since that day when he

23

had killed Roberta Valdez, his life had been aimed in one direction—to help those who didn't know how to help themselves.

"Oh, how did we get off on that dreadful subject!" Edwina shuddered delicately, closing her eyes. "All I'm saying is, you need to get—"

"I know. I need to get married."

"You'll be thirty in August. Thirty." She repeated the number in an unbelieving tone, checking her chin muscles with one hand.

"I'm no spring chicken." Refilling his tea glass he strolled to the edge of the porch, contemplating the setting sun. "Perhaps you're right, Mo—Edwina." A recent feeling of desire, a bit of warm sunshine held in his arms, and a pair of wide brown eyes occupied his thoughts. "With summer coming, maybe I do need to take a little time off and enjoy the sun."

His heart raced as he remembered the golden girl running blithely across the road ahead of his car. His squealing brakes and a roaring in his ears had brought the accident all back to him. Mark remembered how he'd felt twelve years ago, young, lost, wanting only to cry, "Why?" Now he tried to answer that cry for other searching, insecure young people caught in that no-man's land called adolescence. A by-product of his constancy had been election to the state legislature.

Not realizing what he was doing, Mark stared at the grubby envelope in his hand, slowly tearing it open as he thought about his class. The note could be from one of the teens because at each weekly session they wrote notes of encouragement to class members. He unfolded the crumpled sheet. No, not from an ex-class member. The typed note read: Stop Meddling with Liquor Licenses!

He had just returned from a speaking tour all over the

state, urging a bill to make liquor licenses state owned. It wasn't an ideal law but it was a first step in controlling sales to minors. The opposition was apparently launching a scare campaign immediately.

Mark's instinct was to wad the note and trash it, but perhaps he should save it. Who knew what the future held? Battles over bills in the New Mexico Legislature were notoriously hot and emotional. Thoughtfully Mark folded the note, returning it to its rumpled envelope. He didn't have time to think about it now.

Tonight's class opened a new course in Adventures in Living Free. The judge had given Mark a list of seventeen participants, all juveniles and first offenders automatically enrolled at the judge's decree. If they failed to attend the two-hour sessions over the nine-week period, their sentences were reviewed, so attendance was usually good.

Mark used the time before class to set up his room and go over the outline he followed. Then he sat down, preparing himself for the challenge of the evening and praying for those attending. He had to surround himself with a sense of calm to meet the "I'm here, but I'm not going to cooperate" attitude that inevitably faced him in the first sessions. His assistants, graduates of past sessions, arrived soon. They were now admirers of Mark and what he stood for.

"Good. Right on time." He handed each a list of the students enrolled. "Do any of these names look familiar to you?"

Lynn, the young man, scanned the sheet. "Yeah, I know some. Looks like another tough group."

"Aren't they all." Noele raised her eyes expressively, and they shared an understanding grin. "But that's part of the challenge."

"You want me to start the first talk?" Lynn was rereading the instruction guide.

"Fine. Noele can handle the recordkeeping." Mark made a final inspection of the room. "I'll introduce you right after my opening." His eyes rested on the refreshment table.

Anticipating him, Noele suggested, "I'll just make sure we have everything we need for the break."

Lynn was carefully tucking in his shirt and pushing up the sleeves on his jacket. Mark noted the outward signs that he was still a little nervous about speaking to a group of peers who would regard him at first as a turncoat.

"Remember, we start this first session very low-key."

Lynn cleared his throat. "Right."

Noele, seated at the back table, sorted through the enrollment cards she was filling in from the list. "You'll do great, Lynn; don't panic." She smiled her encouragement.

Mark classified this first session as the opening round of "Make me, just try to make me do it." They began with a non-critical atmosphere which only later, about session four, would work its magic. Then the kids would open up and communicate on a feeling level far beyond the usual surface chatter.

During the break Mark stood apart and drank his coffee, intently studying each person. He never made overtures during the first session. One face kept attracting his attention. A slender young man of Hispanic origin, with thick black hair and thin features, stood alone with his hooded black eyes concentrated on Mark. Mark felt he knew that face well, but he couldn't place it. He racked his brain, again glancing at the young man. The knowledge that he should recognize the youth nagged at Mark the remainder of the evening. Where had he seen that face?

As the last notes of the song died on her lips Lisa swiveled on the piano bench to watch her grandmother. The light from the floor lamp, with its richly colored leaded glass lampshade, glinted off Jewel's wire spectacles. Her silver head bobbed in time with her rapidly crocheting fingers.

"There." Tying off the last stitch Jewel held the pink object up to the light. Her wrinkled, work-brittle hands held it gently. "That completes the set: jacket, bonnet, and booties." The two dogs at her feet raised their heads as if examining the articles. Blinking solemn eyes, they replaced their noses between front paws.

"Who is it for?" Lisa fingered the delicate work and was amazed at the hours of labor involved in such a tiny bit of fluff.

"No one." Jewel laughed at her granddaughter's astonished expression. "But sure as the world there will be a baby shower soon for one of the women at church, and I'll have something ready." She folded the tiny garments away. "Play another tune while I just sit. I need to think about something for Kim. Something special for a wedding present." Leaning back in her chair Jewel closed her eyes.

Lisa played softly and listened as Jewel mused, "It's difficult for me to realize Kim's old enough to get married. Seems only yesterday I bandaged scraped knees. Ah well, we grow older every day, don't we?" She sighed. "I hope we grow wiser, too. But I talk too much. Sing an old tune for me."

So Lisa played "The Old Rugged Cross," singing the familiar words to please her grandmother. When she had finished, Lisa thumbed through the hymnal and commented, "The special music chorus practices early Wednesday night. We're doing 'Our God, He Is Alive.'"

"A lovely song." Jewel rocked slowly in her chair waiting for Lisa to try it.

Lisa had finished the first verse when the doorbell rang. "I'll get it."

"Go ahead and practice." Jewel waved Lisa back to the bench. "It's that insurance man, I'm sure. He called earlier. Join us later when you've finished. He might like coffee or something by then." Pressing in her silver waves with one hand and adjusting her glasses with the other, Jewel went to the door. The dogs rose, going with her to inspect the newcomer.

Lisa ran through the chorus and verses several times. The special group practiced every Wednesday evening before regular midweek services. The members were two high school students, a college junior, and two middle-aged women. A professor acted as leader and sang tenor. Lisa hadn't met the other tenor who came, the professor laughingly commented, when he was in town. At home Lisa's parents didn't attend church regularly. But here, Jewel's life revolved around the church, and Lisa indulged her grandmother.

Finally Lisa closed the hymnal and went to the front room. At her entrance a dark, good-looking man stood to meet her. He took both her hands and exclaimed, "Ah! *Señorita*! You sing like a bird."

Pulling her hands free, Lisa responded with a reserved, "Thank you." She looked to her grandmother for guidance in how to react to such Latin exuberance.

Smiling, Jewel introduced them. "Carl Valdez, my granddaughter, Lisa Beall. Carl is here to update my insurance to make you the main beneficiary."

"You shouldn't! I didn't come—" Appalled, Lisa protested strongly.

Jewel's look quelled her. They wouldn't argue the point in front of Mr. Valdez. "Perhaps, Mr. Valdez would like a cup of coffee? And lemon pound cake?"

Lisa, reminded of her duty, asked, "Cream or sugar?"

"Black, thank you. And the lemon cake sounds good." Dark brown eyes soulfully inquired of both ladies, "You will have some too?"

"Only a small piece," specified Jewel to Lisa.

The younger dog, Goldie, followed her in hopes of tidbits. At the kitchen door Lisa paused, the room dark. Just as she flicked the switch to flood the room with light, the weirdest sensation came over her—a feeling of being watched. A low growl from Goldie did nothing to reassure her. Surreptitiously Lisa glanced toward the window but could see nothing. It was only her imagination, she told herself. Tossing her ash blonde hair she turned on the kettle to heat the water for instant coffee. Goldie paced the floor, a low rumbling noise in his throat.

Lisa tried to ignore the feathery tingle up her spine as she sliced the lemon cake, placing it on saucers. Next she added dainty napkins with bluebells bordering the edge, forks, and cups in saucers. With a feeling of escape she carried the tray quickly from the kitchen to the comfortable safety of other humans in the front room. Reluctantly Goldie followed her, but placed himself near the hall door with ears perked.

Carl Valdez closed his briefcase, business concluded. Smiling up at Lisa in admiration he took his coffee and cake. Perhaps because of her relief at being back in their presence, her answering smile encouraged him more than she meant. But, she excused herself as she sipped her coffee, he is a good-looking man.

Remembering her earlier statement that she could handle her own love life, she asked, "What sorts of insurance do you sell, Mr. Valdez?"

"Carl, please. I carry a complete line—car, home, and life. But I concentrate on life insurance."

"Have you always sold life insurance?"

"Twelve years now." He nodded complacently to Jewel.

"Do you have many fraud cases?" This thought had come to Lisa earlier when Jewel informed her of her beneficiary change. How vulnerable an older person could be!

"Why do you ask?" His brown eyes suddenly lost their limpid appeal, becoming deep black dots.

Surprised at his curtness, Lisa assured, "I just wanted to know more about you." Was that flirtatious pause hers? What possessed her? She ignored her grandmother's searching look and raised eyebrow.

"And I you, *Señorita*." The dark eyes once again appraised her. "Perhaps, with your permission, *Señora*, I could take your granddaughter to eat Wednesday evening to become better acquainted? Tonight I must leave." His grimace expressed his feelings. "Another appointment. It is okay?"

Not really desirous of an entire evening alone with Carl Valdez, Lisa hedged, "I'm sorry. This Wednesday night is reserved for midweek services at church."

"Church? Of course, I understand. Another time, then?" He rose, placing his cup on the tray beside Lisa.

When he left they would be alone she realized—with an unknown presence somewhere outside. "Surely you would like a little more coffee?"

Valdez hesitated. "Perhaps a little more."

Only then did Lisa understand that her suggestion involved returning to the kitchen. Did her dismay show on her face? It must have, for Carl asked, "Is something wrong? I could help?"

Help get a cup of coffee? How ridiculous he would think her if she agreed. "No…" her voice faltered. "It will only take a moment. Grandmother? More coffee?"

"No, dear, thank you." Jewel took up her crochet hook. "I've had enough to keep me awake awhile."

Still Lisa delayed. "Anything else, hot tea?"

"No, thanks anyway." Jewel noticed how big Lisa's brown eyes appeared.

Lisa moved toward the hall, smiling faintly. Goldie rose immediately, ready to accompany her. Carl also stood. "I could use a drink of water." He followed her to the kitchen. "Lisa—" Carl only had time to say her name when Goldie sprang at the window.

Dropping the tray with a clatter Lisa screamed, "Carl! Carl!"

At first he thought he had startled her. Then Valdez saw she pointed at the window—at a face framed between the white, red-trimmed curtains. With Goldie barking violently at his heels Carl dashed out the back door in pursuit. Lisa heard crashing of lilac bushes, then silence. She went to the window but could see nothing.

As Lisa knelt to pick up the tray and broken things, Jewel Beall hurried into the kitchen trailing yarn. Gripping Honey's collar and breathing shallowly Jewel demanded, "What's going on? Did he attack you? My dear—"

"No, no. Sorry I frightened you." Quickly Lisa helped Jewel to a chair. "I saw a face in the window. That's what caused all the excitement."

Lisa carefully collected the pottery chips. "When I saw those eyes looking at me, I just froze! I felt a tingling sensation all over my skin as if my hair literally stood on end. A feeling I don't want to relive—ever!"

"And Carl? Where's he?" Jewel held her hand to her chest trying to regain her composure. *If anything hap-*

pened to Lisa! Her heart nearly stopped at the thought.

"He dashed after the man."

Both women turned as Carl entered the kitchen, straightening his tie and dusting his clothes.

"Did you catch him?" Jewel eyed Carl's ruffled appearance.

"He got away. But I frightened him enough that he won't be back."

"I'm so thankful you were here." Lisa's voice trembled.

"So am I!" His response was so fervent Lisa looked at him inquiringly but Carl seemed completely sincere.

"We were certainly fortunate you were here," Jewel added. "You're sure whoever it was is gone?"

Goldie scratched at the back door. Faithful to his duty, he had barked outside until the car left the vicinity. Now he wanted back in for the night. In the living room Carl gathered up his papers and briefcase.

"Thank you again." Lisa repeated.

Carl spoke softly, eyeing Mrs. Beall who was rewinding her yarn. "I think it would be a good idea if I come to pick you up Wednesday evening for the singing and church. And then to bring you home, just as a precaution."

Lisa remembered her frozen, helpless feeling earlier. She thought about two women arriving home after services late Wednesday night. She turned to Jewel. "Carl has suggested he take us to music practice and church day after tomorrow."

"And perhaps coffee and pie at Hobo Joe's after?" he begged charmingly.

Peering at him over her reading glasses, Jewel Beall smiled. "I see you have gotten your way after all."

At her indulgent agreement Carl's smile became smug. "I always get my way."

32

Chapter Three

That night after class as he rounded the last curve back to the ranch, Mark called up the vision of golden loveliness that had dashed into the road earlier. He remembered flashing brown eyes and a defiant chin, and felt a desire to see her, to hold her lithe figure again.

He had half-promised his mother he would stay in Three Rocks for the summer. Lee, his ranch manager, would be delighted. Besides his regular legislative duties, Mark had numerous speaking engagements, but with careful organization he could do it.

Kim met him at the front door. "I thought I heard your car." Tucking her arm in his with a loving squeeze Kim drew him into his study. "I wanted a chance to talk to you alone." She pushed him down on the brown leather couch in front of the fireplace. "First, you must admire my ring!" She waved her hand in his face, then sank on the edge of the glass and wood coffee table before him. "Oh, Mark, it's heavenly being in love and—engaged." She smiled dreamily. "You should try it."

"First Mother, now you." Mark laughed, ruffling her short blonde curls before relaxing against the throw pillows on the couch. "Is this a conspiracy?"

"Mother? What do you mean?"

"She's after me to get married." Quoting his mother, Mark mimicked, "After all, you're getting ancient."

"She wants you to marry that poisonous Sheila Richardson-Baird. Once Mother gets a notion she can't see anything else." For a moment Kim was silent, her chin propped in her hands.

Chuckling at her defense of him, Mark reassured her. "She won't push me into marriage too actively. Grandchildren give ages away so easily."

"Frankly, the idea of children deters me a little, too. Don't you think it's better to wait awhile?" She fingered the brass eagle on the coffee table, tracing the wing design.

"Absolutely." Mark wadded one of the throw pillows under his head and propped his feet on the table. "But the threat of grandchildren always sidetracks Mother when she's backing me into a corner, so I keep it handy."

They both were silent for a while thinking their own thoughts. Finally Kim swallowed. "I wish, just for the summer…" Her voice trailed off wistfully.

"What do you wish, Kim?" A gentle light glowed in his eyes.

"I don't know how to say it exactly." Hesitating, Kim studied her dear, dear brother. He gave so much to life, asking nothing for himself. She wanted him to know a love like the love she and Randal shared. He deserved it. Abruptly she walked over to the mantel and looked back at him stretched out in relaxation. Physically attractive, his eyes held an appealing world-weary air. Women fawned at his feet, but he didn't see them in his quest toward his goals. Somebody needed to bring him up short to make him realize life without love wasn't worth living.

"Well?" Mark raised his eyebrows.

"This summer will be our last…like it has been. I mean, I'll be married in August and then…" Kim paused, trying to make him comprehend. "Then, nothing will ever be the same again. Don't you see?" She crossed to stand before him while she spoke, and he pulled her down beside him on the couch.

"I do understand. Marriage will change things. No longer will you be my kid sister. You'll be a wife, a companion, a lover to your Randal, and eventually, a mother." Mark put his arm around her shoulder and held her close. "Oh yes, there'll be lots of changes. That's God's plan. You must leave us and make your life with Randal."

Kim's sigh was a mixture of bliss and sadness. "And I want to. But, couldn't you…we do some special things together this summer? Couldn't you take a little time off for me?"

Mark sat up on the couch as he came to a decision. "I can, and I will."

"Oh, Mark! You are a sweetie pie!" Kim hugged him exuberantly and began the next phase of her campaign. "For openers, I want you to have lunch with us—me at the club tomorrow."

"Us?" Mark's eyes narrowed, instantly suspicious. One eyebrow rose above his hazel eyes.

Kim paused before springing her surprise. "Jewel's granddaughter." Her announcement brought a gleam of interest.

Settling herself more comfortably on the couch, she continued. "I ran into Lisa on the way to show Jewel my ring." Kim checked to make sure it still sparkled on her finger and took a moment to admire the circle of gold. "She was singing the catchiest melody. Of course, I introduced myself." She gauged Mark's reaction to her tale. "I've asked her to sing in my wedding. She hasn't

35

committed herself, so don't do anything to scare her off."

"Now how could I scare her off?" Mark laughed. "I haven't even met her." Then he frowned. Of course, the young woman in the road had to be Jewel's granddaughter.

"I don't know, but just don't. For one thing, don't tell her you're singing a solo. She might use the excuse that one solo is enough." Kim reverted to her former topic of conversation. "You will, won't you?"

"Will?" Mark's mind was still on the young woman in the road.

"Eat with us at the club tomorrow!" Kim threw up her hands in exasperation.

"Sure." Mark grinned at her antics. He wondered if Jewel's granddaughter knew his identity. Probably not or she wouldn't be planning to eat with Kim, not after their confrontation.

"Good. I'll call Lisa to tell her it's on."

Edwina opened the door. "Here's where you are! Wouldn't you like some coffee? Come to the den and keep us company."

"I could use some coffee." Mark rose, flexing his shoulder muscles and loosening his tie. "It has been a long day."

Linking arms with Kim on one side, he took his mother's arm also, and escorted them to the den. Inez was there working on her needlepoint. Mark wondered what she did with it. He never saw any displayed, yet she always had an article in her hand.

The den also had a fireplace, but here the southern colonial decorations had given way to the Southwest. On the mantel was a collection of western bronzes. Remington prints mingled with originals done by New Mexican artists. The furniture groupings were earth tones, soft and comfortable.

Kim curled up in the corner of the couch to watch the news on television. The announcer was telling of a beer truck hijacked in the northern part of the state. Next a picture of Mark flashed on the screen, followed by a summary of his new bill concerning liquor licenses. The reporter asked, "Could there be a connection between the rash of hijackings and Mark London's proposal?"

Before the others realized his intention, Mark crossed the room and turned off the set. The publicity of the political arena always embarrassed him.

"Oh, this coffee has cooled. You took so long." Edwina impatiently pushed the intercom buzzer. Before the housekeeper answered, a chatter of voices and static was heard in the background. "That Flora," complained Edwina. "She has that CB base station turned so loud she can't hear a thing. Sometimes I wonder why I put up with her."

"Until you taste her barbecue sauce," Kim said.

"And eat her enchiladas," added Mark, taking an easy chair and propping his feet on the ottoman.

"True." Edwina smiled at her own impatience. "But how she can enjoy listening to all those people talking and calling each other silly names is beyond me." She fluttered her hand. "I suppose if it keeps her content out here in the desert I shouldn't complain."

She sighed, and it crossed Mark's mind that she might like to move to a smaller place in town after Kim married. Always before she had protested there wouldn't be room for all her things, but perhaps that was changing.

Edwina switched off the intercom. "Kim, run see about some hot coffee for Mark. I know he must need it after flying in from Santa Fe, then having to rush straight off to that class." But since Mark's class always led to an unpleasant memory, she dropped the subject and spoke of local events.

When Kim returned with the coffee she was surprised by a question from her mother. "What's Jewel Beall's granddaughter like?" Edwina didn't look up from the cards she was laying out for solitaire.

"I'm having lunch with her tomorrow." Kim poured Mark's cup and carried it to him, sharing a conspiratorial smile. "I'll bring her by here after, if you'd like to meet her."

"Do that." Her tone was carefully bland, but Mark and Kim both knew their mother enjoyed knowing all the news. They weren't surprised either that her mind moved on to Kim's wedding.

"One of the first things we must plan is an announcement party. What sort do you have in mind, Kim?"

Surprised that her ideas would be considered, Kim suggested, "Randal would be happier outside, in the afternoon."

"Outside?" Edwina's vision of a large hall, a band, and tables overflowing with food collapsed but was immediately replaced with another. "A garden party. What a delightful idea! You're right. The flowers are lovely now, before the full heat of summer. We could have canopies, flowers everywhere, and white swings. Kimberly, I believe you are inspired! Don't you agree, Inez?" The cards were forgotten.

Inez responded to her cue. "Very good, Kim. A lovely idea."

"Perhaps I was inspired." Kim winked at Mark as she slipped into her shoes. "But right now bed is the only thing on my mind."

"Two weeks from this Thursday." Edwina continued to plan.

"Bed for me, too." Mark stood, placing his cup on the tray.

Flora's appearance in the doorway stopped Edwina's organization. "Yes, Flora?"

"I've come for the tray." Flora was a short, plump, jolly-looking sort of woman until you saw her eyes. Surprisingly blue in her dark Hispanic complexion, they were a hard and businesslike steel color. "It's past my time to be clearing up." Pointedly she picked up Inez's cup and saucer.

"But where's Dulce?" Edwina tried to be conciliatory. "You go on, Flora. She can tend to the tray."

"She's not here." Flora added with a hint of a sneer, "She's always had Monday nights off ever since she was taking Mr. Mark's class."

"I forgot." Edwina didn't want to upset Flora. "We're all through, aren't we?" She smiled nervously.

Kim and Mark agreed in chorus, their usual reaction to Flora. She had a daunting effect on them, both putting them on the defensive and causing them to jump at her commands. Mark puzzled over this power Flora wielded, but he tried to accommodate her because of his mother. Only Inez remained silent, raising her eyes from her work and staring belligerently at Flora. But she too added her napkin to the tray before her. Mark was surprised to catch Inez's small rebellion. Ordinarily Inez was so willing to please, yet her eyes said she hated Flora. Again he glanced at Inez, but her head was lowered, her eyes on her needlework. Had he misinterpreted that gaze? He was intrigued by this sudden glimpse into Inez's personality.

Mark asked, "How is the problem with your nephew Phil?"

Flora had finished collecting the cups and was ready

to leave the room, but at his question she paused in the doorway.

Dropping her needle, Inez found it before meeting his eyes. "Phillip? I'm sure something can be worked out."

Mark could feel undercurrents between the two women, but Kim took his arm and laughed. "You can discuss serious things tomorrow. Come on, I want to ask you something."

Relieved, Inez returned to her work and Flora left. Edwina continued her plans for the garden party. "Seven hundred people. We should settle on a date so I can notify the caterer. And the announcements. Kim, we should do that first thing tomorrow."

But Kim and Mark had started down the hall. Laughing, Kim agreed with her mother, calling back over her shoulder. She didn't stop until she had towed Mark into her private sitting room. Picking up one of the stuffed animals on her white canopy bed, she cuddled it in her arms. "You should be glad I'm getting married," she teased.

Mark strolled across her blue shag carpet to gaze out at the security light where insects fluttered. A guttural sound was his response, but he did glance around and smile.

"All my wedding arrangements should keep her busy, happy, and out of your hair." When he remained silent she settled in a chair covered in a bluebonnet print. "What's on your mind, Mark?"

"Did you notice anything strange between Inez and Flora?" Hands in his pockets, he turned to watch her.

"Nothing except that Flora gives the orders and we all obey." She lightly dismissed his question. "By the way, how was your trip? Did you develop speaker's dry mouth disease?"

"Definitely!" He laughed, going along with her attempt to change his mood. Perhaps he was just tired. Touring and speaking were debilitating. "I've started people thinking, even if negatively." Pulling out the note he had received earlier, he showed it to her.

"Negatively?" Kim unfolded the note. As she read it she left her chair and clutched his arm. "Mark! This isn't just negative—it's a threat!"

He had made a mistake showing her the note. He tried to pass it off by saying in a mock judicial tone, "I thought it sounded a little that way."

But Kim wasn't fooled. "You must be careful!"

"How can I be careful? I've no idea whose fur I've rubbed the wrong way. It could be anyone. Besides, I'm home for the summer with some much needed catching up on the ranch ahead of me."

"You've promised to spend time with me, too, 'member?"

Affectionately Mark flipped her pert nose. "I intend to."

"Then I'm calling Lisa right now, even though it's late, and confirming our lunch date for tomorrow. Still willing?"

"Willing." *More than willing*, Mark added to himself, as he remembered the golden girl he had held in his arms.

Mark read the note through again. Then he returned it to his pocket and put it completely out of his mind. He couldn't worry about every threat that came along. A long time ago he had made the choice to do the best he could in every endeavor. If it meant making enemies, then so be it. Returning to the window he stared at the security light and listened to Kim's telephone conversation.

"Lisa, this is Kim. I was calling—Lisa, what's wrong? You sound near tears!"

Mark stepped closer and raised his eyebrow in query.

"A window peeper!"

Mark started for the door.

"We'll be right over!" Kim assured her, but she signaled Mark to wait. "You're sure he's gone? Carl who? Carl Valdez? *He* was there? What on earth for? Oh, he does sell insurance, doesn't he? You're sure you don't want me to come over?"

Reluctantly Mark returned to the window, his hands stuffed in his pockets, while Kim continued the conversation. "I'll pick you up at twelve and Mark will meet us there. Don't hesitate to call if you need help." As she cradled the receiver Kim grimaced at Mark. "You heard? A window peeper."

"I heard a very lopsided account. Why was Carl there?"

"Carl carries Jewel's policies. Fortunately, he was on hand to chase the window peeper away." Kim narrowed her eyes as she thought about Carl.

"Old Carl to the rescue," muttered Mark, running a hand through his hair. He was silent a moment, then asked, "Twelve tomorrow at the club?"

"Right."

"Goodnight then." After a quick hug Mark touseled Kim's curls and left. But he didn't go directly to his room. Downstairs he wandered out on the patio. Darkness had brought a cooling breeze. The hum of buzzing insects made a background melody to his thoughts.

He strolled through a break in the japonica hedge in the backyard. Easily slipping through, he followed the old trail in the moonlight. He had traversed this trail regularly over the last twenty-odd years.

As a young boy exploring this terrain he had immediately discovered James and Jewel Beall and their gracious lifestyle. After her husband died, Jewel leased her ranch to Mark's father; now she leased it to Mark. In that one small way he could help her in return for all her love and understanding over the years.

Now, Jewel's granddaughter had come to live with her. A window peeper! He couldn't sleep without assuring himself that the intruder had indeed gone, that all was well.

Mark stood outside the yard in the shadow of a tree and studied the house and grounds. While he watched, light after light switched off. Finally the light in the southeast bedroom blinked out.

He thought again of the golden girl he had held in his arms that day. Radiant, alive, impetuous, lovely. And she had given him the fright of his life! The memory brought into vivid focus that other night years ago when he had run down Roberta Valdez.

Tonight Carl Valdez had been here at the Beall house when the prowler appeared. Carl Valdez—Roberta's husband.

An involuntary shiver overcame Mark as he stood in the darkness. Why was that spectre from his past haunting him again? He saw the running figure, heard the dull thud, and saw Carl staring at the body on the roadside, broken bottle in his hand. And, Mark saw Roberta's small brother clutching her close, sobbing his heart out.

Then Mark knew why that young, dark-eyed man in his Adventures class tonight had seemed so familiar. He was that boy, grown and needing help.

Chapter Four

"That's the Guadalupe range to the southwest." Kim waved at the vista as they topped a small rise on their way to the club the next day. "Beautiful country. It truly is 'the land of enchantment.' " Kim's delight validated the state slogan.

"It is enchanting, isn't it?" Lisa thought how sticky-hot her Oklahoma home would be now. "A strange, compelling sort of beauty. Not gaudy with trees and gigantic flowers in profusion, but subtle. I don't know that I can express my feelings." She smoothed out an imaginary wrinkle in her hand-embroidered muslin smock dress. "When a wildflower does grow and survive out here, it's a special, enduring sort of loveliness."

Kim smiled across at Lisa. "I hope you stay long enough to learn about this land and its people." Then Kim brought up the subject uppermost in her mind. "On Saturday *my darling Randal* will be here." Grinning impishly she emphasized the words, making Lisa laugh. "Anyway, with Mark we can make a foursome and have tennis doubles and a picnic. Sound okay?"

"Tennis? I'd love to! I haven't played in two months." She counted up the time in surprise.

"Here we are." Kim parked the Pinto, and they

crossed the lot, the asphalt hot beneath their sandals. The golf green rolled away to their left and behind the one-story club building. "If you don't have anything to do this afternoon, we could play a set or so to limber you up," offered Kim, tucking the car keys into the pocket of her peach wraparound skirt. "Mother wants to meet you too."

"Sounds great!" Lisa tugged on the black wrought iron handle of the massive double doors at the club entrance. "I need the exercise since my change of routine." Ruefully she glanced down at her trim figure. "I don't want to outgrow my clothes while I'm here."

"Big worry!" Laughing together they passed through the reception room. The club was beautifully furnished in peach, navy, and brown tones. Kim led the way to the dining room where a long table with warming pans was the main attraction. Between introductions to Kim's friends and their sudden exclamations over the flashing solitaire on her finger, the two girls had trouble filling their plates.

Finally they made their way to a table occupied by an attractive woman who had beckoned Kim to join her.

"Lisa, this is Ann Nix, local reporter. Ann, meet my new neighbor, Lisa Beall, Jewel Beall's granddaughter."

Ann smiled, "Glad to—"

Kim let out an ecstatic yell, "Mark! You did come!"

Startled, Lisa tilted her plate slightly, dropping a pimento-stuffed green olive on the floor. It continued its journey across the hardwood to stop at a pair of brown boots. Raising her eyes from the boots, Lisa encountered familiar hazel eyes that seemed to mock, "Got you at last!" So this was brother Mark.

Although he no longer wore the perfectly cut dress suit, she recognized him instantly as the man in the road. Today he was clad in tight-fitting jeans. A white

45

short-sleeved Western shirt accented his tan.

He spoke to Kim. "Lee had an errand in town and dropped me off here."

Lisa's brief smile at Kim's introduction managed to appear disinterested, but it had nothing to do with her reaction to the man. In his presence she felt once again a warm surging in her veins, a sudden heightening of her senses.

While Mark filled his plate at the buffet, Kim answered Ann's probing questions about Randal and her engagement. Then Ann's questions moved on to Mark and his activities. "Has there been any backlash on Mark's new bill for state-owned liquor establishments?" Kim didn't mention the threatening note Mark had received. In a small town everybody knew too much anyway.

Ann's interest in Mark gave Lisa a needed moment to compose herself. "How did your speaking tour go?" Ann tried to dig information from Mark, but he laughed and concentrated on his food.

Ann gave up and focused her attention on Lisa. "I did understand Kim to say you're Jewel Beall's granddaughter, didn't I?"

Nodding and smiling, Lisa felt a flash of pride in the relationship.

"Are you visiting or do you plan to stay? Career plans?" Her barrage gave Lisa no time to respond. At her expression of dismay, Ann laughed. "How can I discover anything if I don't ask?" Kindly she added, "Answer only what you want to."

"I graduated in May, in need of rest and recovery, so here I am." No need to mention her grandmother's failing health nor her own uncertain future.

"She's going to sing in my wedding. She writes songs, too."

46

Lisa appreciated Kim's praise. It gave her more confidence, which she needed at the moment, but it also whetted Ann's interest. "Did you sing in a group?"

"Yes I did," she replied slowly. She wondered why she wasn't proud of this accomplishment when she thought of the members of the band.

"What sort?"

Mark paused momentarily in his eating, then continued.

Piqued at his seeming absorption with food Lisa ignored him and answered Ann. "We sang a little bit of everything." Ann and Kim didn't even pretend to eat.

"I was with a group named The Wind." *Was?* Lisa wondered at her use of the past tense. "We sang for all the sorority dances and such. And—" She found herself still trying to get a reaction from Mr. Know-it-all. "We put out two records that are doing well."

"You have?" Kim sounded more surprised than awed. But there was no misreading Mark's expression as it changed from disappointment to disdain. Why was he disappointed in her? What had he expected? She had failed in some way.

Smiling brilliantly to hide her own hurt and confusion, Lisa took a large bite so she couldn't respond to any more of Ann's questions. Like a turtle she retreated into her shell and hoped things would be better the next time she emerged.

But Ann enthusiastically pursued the lead. "Could I come out and do a feature story on you? George Mahon at the TV station might want you on his talk show, too."

Ann's eagerness soothed Lisa's spirit. "Come out anytime."

"Do you plan to make any more records?"

"We've considered it." Lisa didn't want to express her reservations. "There are lots of considerations—"

47

"I should think so!" Mark burst out. "What sort of here and there life would you live? Don't you know where that path would lead you?" A downward stab of his fork to indicate the direction stunned them all to silence.

Lisa seethed at his dictatorial manner. But she had known what he was like, hadn't she? Somehow, the penetrating eyes, his tall, athletic figure, his firm, strong features and waving brown hair had made her forget that aspect of his personality.

Fortunately Ann Nix had finished her meal. Rising, she apologized, "I have an interview at two. Kim, Mark, good to see you. Lisa, so nice to meet you. I'll call soon."

As the silence grew Kim cleared her throat. "Lovely day, isn't it?" Mischievously she wrinkled her nose at the other two, and they all laughed together. The air cleared.

"What delayed you, Mark?" Kim asked.

"Lee was showing me over the ranch, catching me up on projects." For the first time since his outburst his eyes met Lisa's. They were compelling, but he kept the conversation general. "I need to hire a couple of hands to clear up the grounds so everything will be in shape for the garden party."

"Mother!" Kim indulgently smiled. "Which reminds me, Lisa. You're invited to the announcement party whenever she decides on a date." Toying with her spoon, Kim unconsciously lowered her voice. "Did you have any more disturbances last night?"

"No—" Lisa drawled out the word.

"What do you mean?" Kim caught her hesitant response.

"A little after you called, the dogs wanted out."

Mark concentrated on his cucumber salad, feeling

48

conspicuous. The dogs had probably sensed his presence in the yard. He asked, "Did you get a good look at the prowler? Would you recognize him?"

"Yes and no." Lisa shook her head ruefully. "I was so petrified that my mind didn't operate. I do know he was blonde, Anglo, and looked almost as surprised as I was to see someone."

"If you do spot him, let me know!" He snapped the order like a drill sergeant.

"Aye, aye, sir," Lisa mocked with a laugh.

Their eyes met, and Mark's eyes seemed to draw her to them, commanding quiet acquiescence. Lisa lowered her lashes and tried to focus on her plate, bringing back the people, the noise.

Abruptly pushing back his chair, Mark rose. "If you're ready, I am."

Hastily Kim and Lisa followed him out. Kim explained, "We're going to play tennis, so we need to stop and get Lisa's things."

"Fine." Mark held out his hand peremptorily as he opened the passenger side of the car. "I'll drive. Keys."

Kim didn't protest. "I'll ride shotgun." Pushing Lisa into the center, Kim took the window seat. In the small car, Lisa felt scrunched between the two Londons—Kim, friendly and spontaneous on her right; Mark, dogmatic and disapproving on her left.

Mark drove steadily, purposefully, and never above the speed limit, and Lisa wondered if he really *hadn't* been speeding yesterday when he came upon her in the road.

When they reached the Beall ranch, Mark turned in between the gateposts with their large cast iron bells. As in the back garden, Mexican clay bells hung from the trees. A small brass bell hung beside the front door.

Jewel was sitting on the front step, weakly fanning herself. Even from the car she looked pale and ill. Although Lisa had been seated in the middle of the front seat, she was the first to reach her.

"Grandmother! What have you been doing?"

Jewel fluttered a hand as if to smooth a silver wave, but it was too much effort.

Lisa knelt beside her. "Shall I get water? Do you need a tablet?"

Color gradually returned to Jewel's face as she took a deep breath. "Just need a little rest." She managed a smile. "Perhaps I did overdo."

"Drink this." Mark had taken steps immediately and poured water into the glass on the table. He helped Jewel drink as he would a small child.

"Mark!" Jewel's eyes glowed with joy as she relaxed against his supporting arm. "You're home."

"Yesterday, but don't talk." Gently he held her closer to his strength. Lisa and Kim stood by anxiously.

After a moment, Jewel sat up straighter. "I'm feeling better already. Why haven't you been to see me, if you got in yesterday?"

"Actually," admitted Mark, indulgently reassuring her, "I strolled over last night but—" The rest of his explanation was lost as the two dogs bounded around the corner, yelping and leaping on him in excitement.

Startled, Jewel raised white eyebrows. "Were you our window peeper?"

"Sit." The dogs immediately obeyed Mark's command and he began to smooth their shiny long fur as he answered, "No. I wish I'd been here to catch him. When Kim learned about the excitement I came over to check it out, but all was quiet."

Jewel sipped some more water, then tried to get up.

"I'll help you inside." Mark stood to assist her. "You

need to lie down for a while before you start anything else."

"I hate to admit it, but you're probably right." Although her color was better, a tinge of blue still rimmed her lips. She reached out a hand for support. "These old bones give way unexpectedly."

With Mark on one side and Lisa on the other, they steered her up the steps into the cool screened porch. They settled her on a wicker chaise lounge near a telephone.

Kim puffed the pillows, trying in small ways to assist. "It's lucky we came when we did. We stopped so Lisa could get her tennis clothes."

"Go ahead with your plans." Jewel used her 'don't contradict me' tone. "I'm perfectly all right."

Lisa shook her head in protest. "I wouldn't think of leaving you now." She sat on a stool near the lounge.

"I'll be more upset if you stay and miss your fun." Jewel raised herself up. "I'd be heartsick if I thought I made you miss out on playing with Mark and Kim."

Starting to protest again, Lisa saw that Jewel was getting agitated and meant what she said.

Mark confirmed Jewel's self-assessment. "She really will be okay."

"We'll only play awhile, and you can come back to check on her," added Kim.

"Will you stay right there?" Lisa held Jewel's hand tenderly.

"If you'll bring my Bible so I can read a bit."

"I'll get her Bible; you go change," suggested Kim.

In her room Lisa quickly pulled on a white halter-style tennis dress. As she stepped into the accompanying shorts, she wished for a better tan. She tied her hair at the nape of her neck and hurried to the porch, carrying her footlets and Adidas in one hand, her Wilson racket in the other.

"You're ready! Great!" Kim jumped up from her chair.

Mark rose also at Lisa's arrival and her eyes sought his. But once again she discerned disappointment there. What had she done now to bring that look? Hurt and angry, Lisa valiantly covered her feelings by kissing her grandmother's cheek and assuring her she would return soon.

Mark let them out in front of the London house and drove off to the garage. After the hot May sun, the entrance hall felt cool to Lisa. With its white pillars, broad central stair, and air of elegance, the house made Lisa feel she had stepped into something straight out of *Gone with the Wind*. The shrill sound of voices raised in argument broke the illusion of the past.

"Are you accusing me of stealing, Madam? Easily I will find another position!"

"Of course not, Flora." Edwina apologized. "I was excited, overwrought. But my diamond pendant *is* missing. It was a gift from my husband. I placed it on my dresser and now it's gone."

"But I did not take it. Have you spoken to Dulce?" Spitefully the housekeeper added, "With her jail record, I would think she might have an idea. She was instructed to dust this morning."

"Dulce. Of course. Mark insisted I hire her."

Feeling like eavesdroppers, Kim and Lisa shared a glance and stepped backward to leave. Just then Edwina entered from the kitchen, calling Dulce. The maid hurried to answer her call, carrying a dustrag and a bottle of furniture oil. A small Hispanic girl of about sixteen, she had glossy dark hair and big black eyes.

52

Unaware of others, Edwina demanded, "Dulce, what did you do with my diamond pendant?"

"*Señora*, your beautiful pendant? It was there when I dusted your dresser this morning, so bright and sparkling on its velvet cushion."

"It's not there now!" Putting a hand to her throat and taking a deep breath, Edwina continued, "I should have known better than to let Mark hire you!" She closed her eyes and spoke in self-pitying accents.

"*Señora*, Mrs. London." Dulce appealed for understanding. Before she could say anything more, Mark strode rapidly across the hall.

"Mother—Edwina, you can't accuse Dulce without proof." Putting a supporting arm around her he spoke in a soothing tone.

"When I went up just now to put it on, it wasn't there. It has been stolen, I tell you. Stolen!" Edwina pointed at Dulce. "Who else could it be? Flora has been here over a year." Seeing Inez descending the stairs she added, "And Inez was the only other person in the house."

"Mr. Mark, I didn't take it. I promise!" Dulce twisted her hands in her skirt, her eyes dark pools of misery. "You know I would not, not after what you have done for me."

"I'm sure the pendant will turn up. Most likely it has just been mislaid."

Edwina drew herself up in righteous indignation. "You take her word against mine?" Placing her hands together to stop their trembling she declared, "I won't have it! The pendant has been stolen. She stole it. She can't work here any more!"

"*Señora*," begged Dulce. Then realizing Mark had the final say she turned to him. "Mr. Mark, I must work, for my brothers and sisters."

Dulce's impassioned plea brought a lump to Lisa's throat. She looked at Mark. The decision was his. His mother or Dulce?

For a moment Mark looked stymied; then his glance swung past Kim and Inez to Lisa.

Wouldn't you know! Corner him and he turns to me for help! After he condemned my singing career, why should I help him? She hesitated. But then the thought of a perfect solution made her say, "My grandmother needs some extra help. Dulce would be perfect. Then I wouldn't worry about leaving, like this afternoon."

"I knew—thank you." His hazel eyes rewarded her with admiration and respect. "Dulce, I'll take you over right now to talk to Mrs. Beall."

Edwina gazed at Lisa in amazement, suddenly realizing who she was. She took in the bare back, the brief skirt, the long expanse of leg. "You certainly don't dress like a granddaughter of hers, but your misplaced charity convinces me."

Lisa felt heat rising in her at the arrogant censure of another member of the London family. Anger sparked in the deep brown of her eyes. Her mouth opened but she never spoke. Mark was giving orders.

"Dulce, run get your things." He turned to Kim and Lisa, "You two get your tennis game started."

For a strained second, Lisa couldn't move: her hands were tightly clenched and her anger so alive. Kim's sympathetic touch on her arm made Lisa blink. She stopped the tears that welled in her eyes by force of will.

"This hasn't found my pendant," Edwina reminded Mark. "However, I don't have time to discuss it. I'm late already for the Bridge club."

Lisa and Kim didn't stay on the court long. Lisa

couldn't keep her mind on the game and Kim also seemed lost in thought. So, after forty minutes they called a halt. Refusing Kim's offer of a ride, Lisa ran back home through the pasture.

Today she had not had time for singing nor was she in the mood. Hurrying through the gap in the back hedge she almost ran over a young man talking excitedly to Inez. At the sight of her, their conversation ceased.

"Excuse me. I wasn't watching where I was going."

Neither spoke, but both stared at her pointedly, waiting for her to depart.

Turning, Lisa dashed along the path in instinctive flight from their rudeness. She was breathless from her run when she reached the house. "Where are you?" she called. "I'm back."

"Here, Lisa, on the front porch as I promised."

Lisa pointed to the tray containing tall glasses of ice and a few cookies. "You've been up, piddling around."

"Looks that way." Jewel took Lisa's hand in hers and leaned back against her pillows. "Mark was just here with Dulce. She fixed the tray." Jewel looked slightly guilty. "She'll begin tomorrow."

"Did he explain the circumstances?"

"I understand Mrs. London is missing a pendant. But Mark is certain Dulce didn't take it." Thoughtfully she sipped her tea, then pursed her lips. "If Mark is sure, so am I."

"I'm glad he told you." Lisa took a full tea glass from the tray and sat in a wicker chair near Jewel.

Smiling proudly at her granddaughter, Jewel said, "I'm pleased you thought of it."

So Mark had told her that too. Remembering the scene in the Londons' entrance hall, Lisa rose to move restlessly around the porch, unnecessarily straightening things. "My misplaced charity was just like yours Mrs. London said."

Picking up a pillow with intricate crewel work, Lisa traced the design with one finger. "Mrs. London said something else too. She said my clothes didn't look like something a granddaughter of yours would wear."

As she stood before Jewel and glanced down at the skimpy halter, seeing herself through the eyes of the older woman, she didn't need to ask why.

Jewel fiddled with her tea, adding more sugar, her eyes concentrated on stirring. "Well, I suppose it's because I'm so conservative. And I don't play Bridge!" She smiled.

Lisa still felt hurt by Edwina's jeering tone. As if it were relevant she said, "Kim and I didn't play long."

Jewel smiled sadly. "Edwina is jealous of my influence on Mark and Kim. But she was going through a bad time with her nerves, and they needed a friend. How I love the two of them, almost as if they were my own."

Feeling a twinge of jealousy herself at Jewel's admission, Lisa could sympathize with Edwina's emotion. Lisa was also irked that she hadn't realized Jewel Beall's beliefs commanded the respect of those she came in contact with. Her conservatism wasn't something to smile gently about in a knowing way.

"To see Mark now—confident, sure of the direction of his life—makes it difficult to remember how lost and alone he was. He had everything a boy could want, except a real friend." Jewel's eyes closed as she saw again the boy who had become a man with a purpose.

Mark, Mark! thought Lisa in irritation, remembering the disillusionment in his eyes. She was angry with herself because she couldn't banish the memory.

Fortunately Jewel changed the subject. "Drink your tea and tell me about your tennis game."

Although today hadn't been great, tennis was something she could discuss with enthusiasm. "I'm glad we limited ourselves today. I'll be sore enough." Sipping her cold tea she thought about Inez and the young man she had disturbed. "Grandmother, who is Inez?"

"She's Edwina's cousin, somehow. Edwina didn't like being in that big house alone, with Mark in and out and Kim away at college."

But who was the young man? Lisa thought. "I'm heading for the shower." Picking up the tray, she asked, "What should I fix for supper?"

"I thought a fresh spinach salad would do tonight. Remember, Carl Valdez is taking us to church and out afterwards on Wednesday."

"Are you sure you should go tomorrow? Perhaps you should rest."

"Nothing will make me feel as good as going to church, and with the chorus and Mark and Kim maybe you won't be bored this summer."

Lisa laughed at Jewel's worried frown. "Silly. I like being here." She paused before adding, "More than I ever thought I would. How's that for honesty?" Again she laughed, but there could be no mistaking her sincerity.

"I'm glad, very glad." Jewel leaned back on the lounge and closed her eyes. Her lips curved up in a smile.

The late afternoon sun still hung hot and high when Carl Valdez picked them up in his TransAm, glistening black with a gold eagle adorning the hood. Jewel rode in the front of the two-door car, and Lisa took a back seat.

"We practice in the small chapel," said Lisa. "I'm afraid you'll have to listen to us."

"I'll enjoy it." Carl caught her hand to pull her out of the back seat. With a suggestive gleam in his eyes he added. "If not the singing, then watching you." His glance took in her attractive figure and lime-green skirt and blouse. She laughed lightly at his compliment but tugged her hand free and walked beside Jewel into the chapel.

Several members of the chorus were already warming up. Jewel and Carl took inconspicuous places near the back as Lisa found a songbook and joined the others. While they were getting their pitch, Mark and their leader, Larry Goldstein, entered the room.

"Mark," said Goldstein, "meet the newest member of our group, Lisa Beall. Lisa, our missing tenor, Mark London."

To her surprise, Mark took her hand as if they were strangers. "Why, I believe we're neighbors!" He drowned out her hesitant, "We've met," as she tried to pull her hand free.

"Such good neighbors—" he said, squeezing her hand so she had to raise her eyes to meet his, "I can pick Lisa up to sing for the funeral tomorrow."

Others in the group broke in. "Funeral? Tomorrow?"

"One of the women at the nursing home," explained Goldstein. "Tomorrow afternoon at three. Any conflicts? Then be here thirty minutes early to run through the selected songs."

As they sang the swiftly moving hymn, "Our God, He Is Alive," Lisa couldn't stop shivers tingling down her spine. But her mind would not accept some of the words. For now, though, it was enough just to join the swelling chorus.

Joining her grandmother and Carl when the chorus finished, Lisa entered the large auditorium for the mid-week service. Mark London directed the singing. By now Lisa wasn't even surprised. The know-it-all man turned up everywhere and did, indeed, seem to know it all.

Chapter Five

As Lisa and Jewel were preparing for bed that night, Jewel said brightly, "After church Mark told me he'd pick you up at two-fifteen for the funeral. Kim will come for me later. Isn't that sweet of them?" She smiled tenderly. "They're so thoughtful."

Thoughtful? Lisa's word for Mark would have been *conniving*. But the thought that he would go to such effort evoked a tiny bit of joy inside.

The next afternoon she deliberated about what to wear. She assured herself she didn't care a penny what Mark thought but she did want to be dressed properly for the funeral.

Finally she chose a black and white crisp linen dress trimmed with white lace around the collar and cuffs. She wore black hose and, because they would remain standing in the alcove to sing during the funeral service, low-heeled black patent pumps. Lisa tried to be ready when Mark arrived, but he foiled her by arriving early to visit with Jewel. When she joined them in the living room they were laughing congenially.

At her entrance, Mark rose. "Ready?"

Old-fashioned manners to please Jewel, thought Lisa

as she gathered her defenses against the hypnotic hazel brown eyes appraising her.

"Thank you, Mark." Jewel took up her glasses to begin reading after they left. "I know I'm foolish to worry about her going alone. But I do."

"No trouble." Mark held the screen door open for Lisa. "Kim will be along for you in forty minutes or so."

Striding ahead of Mark to his car in an effort to assert her independence, she was easily overtaken. Then, perversely determined not to thank him for his assistance with the car door, Lisa stared straight ahead. The door closed, the key was stuck in the ignition, but Mark made no move to start the engine.

Finally, curiosity won. Turning to see the reason for the delay she found Mark watching her, a smiling curve to his lips—a lazy sort of effort, the tawny eyes shadowed. He looked so innocent, so handsome that Lisa couldn't help a returning smile.

Then, berating herself for her quickly crumbling defenses, she accused, "You didn't ask me, you simply told Jewel I was riding with you."

"I know." His smile became even more beguiling. "Very underhanded maneuver. I was afraid you would refuse me, so I resorted to strategy."

"You could have gone on to work from the funeral, and now you'll have to bring me home. No, I can come back with Kim and Grandmother."

"Lisa," Mark reached across the stick shift and caught her hand. Her eyes had strayed from his, as she tried to keep her senses steady. She pulled away from the shock of feeling his strong hand on hers, but her eyes met his gaze.

"Lisa, you're not listening. I wanted to come by for you. I wanted to…apologize."

"Apologize?" She gave him her full attention now.

"I lost my temper that day...on the road. You startled me." His eyes closed momentarily. "But that's no excuse, really. And for later," he added as an afterthought. Lisa took that for an oblique reference to lunch at the country club.

He put both arms on top of the steering wheel but turned to her. "Forgive me?"

How could she refuse an apology accompanied by that smile—enchanting and contrite all in one? Lisa smiled, dimples on display. Afraid of complete capitulation she qualified, "This time."

Then he started the car, switching on the radio as a background to their conversation. Adeptly Mark questioned her about her family, her interests, and her goals. When they stopped in front of the church, Lisa was surprised. The distance had seemed so short.

As Mark reached to turn off the key, they heard the radio announcer say:

One final item of local interest. Last night two thousand cases of beer were stolen from the Three Rocks warehouse. Police are investigating, and a company representative has announced a one-thousand-dollar reward for information leading to convictions in the crime. Well folks, I hear they pay a fantastic price for this brand on the east coast. Now, for an afternoon of easy listening, stay tuned to KRIM on the Caprock.

Mark commented, "How could you get away with something like that without a man on the inside?"

"Where could you hide that much beer?" Lisa considered the possibilities. "This is wide open land, but at least until roadblocks were removed you'd have trouble."

"You have the mind of a master criminal." Mark laughed.

But she shook her head as he opened her door. "It sounds more difficult than working. I suppose part of the fun is the thrill of danger."

"Many of my students say they felt really alive at such times—with their lives in danger." He placed a hand at her waist to escort her up the walk. He spoke slowly, "I believe that's because they have no purpose for living and feel dead, dead, dead inside. I know that feeling." His fingers tightened around her elbow, and she glanced up to see grim depths in his eyes.

Lisa longed to ask him how he knew, but they were inside the church now. The others were ready to practice the songs they would sing for the funeral in thirty minutes.

The last hymn they sang, "Be with Me, Lord—I cannot live without Thee," had such a compelling melody it repeated itself in her brain. Of course, she had never felt the need of an abiding presence, but it was a comforting thought.

When the funeral was over and they were standing outside, Lisa commented on the large crowd of people. Mark explained that the deceased woman had had eight children and forty-six grandchildren.

"Nothing's sadder than a funeral of an older person who had no children and all of whose contemporaries have already died. At a funeral like that I decide—" He paused to be sure he had Lisa's notice and finished, "that I'm going to have four or five children at least."

"Depending, of course," Lisa provocatively raised an eyebrow. "Depending on what your wife thought about such a plan."

"Perhaps that should be one of the first questions I ask the women I meet." Speaking in a subdued yet joking manner he asked an imaginary woman, "And what, my dear, do you think of producing five offspring? And you?" He pretended to bow in acknowledgement around a circle of women. "And you?" Now he faced Lisa.

How neatly he had turned the tables! Flushing she laughed softly at his foolishness, then shushed him. "Here come the family."

As the procession of cars formed to go to the cemetery, Jewel asked to attend the graveside service.

Lisa, suddenly realizing that she had forgotten her earlier resolve to remain firm against Mark's charm, saw this as an opportunity to escape his company. "I'm sure Mark needs to be at work, so I'll accompany you and Kim."

Mark's eyes narrowed, but he shrugged. "If that's what you want."

Her chin lifted and she stated in a challenging tone, "I don't have to be home until Ann Nix comes at five for an interview."

"I see." His jaw tightened and the yellow flecks disappeared into dusky brown as his pupils darkened.

"Do you?" Pertly she mocked the tone of his earlier question.

"I think I do." The words were even and very quiet. Turning to Mrs. Beall and Kim, he said. "I have things to do in town. See ya." Casually he waved and was gone.

As they waited for the graveside service to begin, Lisa had time to regret her impetuous decision. Why did her hackles rise when she was with Mark London? Of course, his complete confidence in what he was doing and where he was going irked her, since she seemed tossed about in the winds of chance. How could anyone be so certain of his purpose here on earth? Without Lisa's realizing it the service had begun. The minister read his opening text from First Corinthians.

O Death, where is your sting?
O Hades, where is your victory?
The sting of death is sin, and the strength of sin is the law. But thanks be to God who gives us the victory through our Lord Jesus Christ.

Therefore, my beloved brethren, be steadfast, immovable, always abounding in the work of the Lord, knowing that your labor is not in vain in the Lord.

The words penetrated Lisa's thoughts. They seemed to fit in so well with her pondering. Mark stood firm and steady, doing his work, knowing it would be worthwhile because it was in the Lord's service.

She envied him his absolute assurance. But then, that was why she had agreed to come live with her grandmother this summer. She needed to take stock, to meditate, to contemplate her goals, so she could be sure her choice was the correct one.

Did she seriously want to make it in the entertainment field? When applause was ringing in her ears, Lisa had no doubts.

After the applause died away, niggling qualms appeared. The life of a professional performer was such an unstable existence, so ephemeral, often requiring moral compromises, and, in the end, usually sordid. But these anxieties disappeared in the glow of stage lights, in the clamor of approval.

"Give me your arm, dear." Jewel reached for Lisa. "This ground is rough. While we're here I'd like to check on Jim's grave."

The crowd was dispersing now, driving away, leaving the canopy and the mound of flowers as the final tribute to an old woman. Until now Lisa hadn't realized this might be an ordeal for Jewel. Attentive now to her grandmother Lisa broke the silence. "Why so quiet, Kim?"

"I was just thinking…" She glanced at Jewel and didn't finish her sentence.

"Barbaric." Jewel nodded understandingly.

Kim and Lisa agreed they had been thinking the same thing.

"When my Jim died, he didn't want it. A pine box, he said, and keep it simple. I tried."

Lisa remembered with regret she had been on a singing engagement when he died. "Why did you come today, if you didn't want to?"

"It comforts the family to know she had friends. I greatly respected her." They stood before a simple stone and were silent. After a moment Jewel cleared her throat. "I'm ready to go now."

As they helped her across the Bermuda grass and gravel drive Jewel had to pause to wipe her eyes. "I know and you know there's nothing in the ground but dust—my Jim's gone to Heaven. But somehow I get a close feeling just standing there. What a mass of contradictions people are!" Through her tears she laughed at her own inconsistencies.

A mass of contradictions, indeed, agreed Lisa. That defined well her inner turmoil. *A mass of contradictions*. To her the phrase seemed profound.

When she reached the car, Jewel held on to the door. "I think the reason I feel this way is that a cemetery, a funeral, brings the whole cycle of life before me. Being born, living, dying."

Kim sighed. "It makes you look again at all your decisions, like getting married."

"A big decision." Jewel patted Kim's hand, sympathy and love in her touch. "A life decision."

"Yes," agreed Kim. "For better or worse."

How truly her grandmother had spoken! Lisa leaned forward and whispered to her mirror image, "What a mass of contradictions people are!" It was Saturday and she and Mr. Mark London were going to play tennis with Kim and Randal.

"What I'd like to do, as you well know," she insisted to her skeptical reflection, "is work on my song." Since her interview with Ann Nix, she had been inspired to work. But she had been unable to settle down to it.

With Dulce coming to clean she had even more time. Again she checked the mirror to be certain the red culottes fit as they should, tucking the white knit shirt into the waistband. Neither her grandmother nor Mark could fault her outfit. A white hat with red cellophane visor, tilted at a cocky angle, slanted over her brown eyes.

Humming her tune Lisa joined the others on the screened-in porch. Eagerly Kim introduced her to Randal.

He shook her hand firmly with a simple, "Howdy."

They chatted a few minutes; then Jewel asked Randal about his farm operation. "What are you concentrating on this year? Cotton? Wheat?"

"I'm diversifying this year." He continued with his slow drawling voice. Lisa listened, fascinated by the way he seemed to hang on to each word. "Cotton prices are high but the wheat is low. Sunflowers mess up the soil, but the market's steady on them." He tucked his hands in the pockets of his tennis shorts. It was obvious he was more comfortable in Levi's.

"Any corn?" Mark wasn't so tanned as Randal, but he looked superb in tennis casuals—tall, well-built, muscles firm.

"Water table's too low. Takes lots."

"Doesn't it though." Jewel chuckled. "My Jim used to say you put fish in the irrigation rows and keep them alive all summer to raise a crop of corn."

They all laughed at this; then Jewel picked up her knitting needles. "You've pandered to me long enough; run along and have fun." She waved them off with a final warning. "Now don't stay out in this sun too long."

Feeling guilty that she'd already forgotten her grandmother's suggestion to use sun screen, Lisa immediately tugged it from her racket case and spread it down her arms.

Kim held out her hand as they followed the men around the back of the house to the path leading to the Londons. "Some for me, too?"

An indulgent smile crinkled Jewel's eyes. She called after them, "One of the privileges of being old is giving out orders."

When they reached the gate at the back, Randal and Kim took the lead and Mark waited for Lisa.

Thinking about her grandmother Lisa said, "I hope I grow old as gracefully."

"She's a saint." Mark took Lisa's tennis bag. "A light set on a hill."

Kim looked back over her shoulder. "The courts at the club are better, but everyone would want to meet Randal." She tucked her arm in his. "Selfishly I wanted this time just for us."

"Me, too." A flush darkened Randal's tan and showed pink on his forehead where he usually wore a hat. He pulled Kim closer.

Laughing up at him, Kim added. "They can meet you at the garden party."

For a while they stayed together, Mark sounding out Randal, asking more about his farm, family, and interests. Soon, however, with surprising adroitness Randal managed to separate the group as he and Kim moved on ahead.

Mark seemed preoccupied, so Lisa remained silent, letting the beauty of the day soak in. The sun was so bright that even with sunglasses she had to shade her eyes to look off in the distance.

"How gorgeous!" Lisa couldn't stop her involuntary exclamation. There beside the path was a prickly pear cactus in full bloom, the exotic purple-pink flower a miracle of the desert.

Tilting her sunglasses into her hair, Lisa knelt near the plant and with glowing eyes, looked up at Mark. "I'm glad we came this way today; otherwise I might have missed it."

He knelt beside her and wistfully touched the smooth petals, avoiding the thorns. "Such fleeting beauty." For a moment they silently paid tribute. As they stood, Mark smiled slowly, and said, "I'm glad I came this way, too."

Thinking perhaps he was mocking her, Lisa bristled. But his gaze was now on the horizon. "Our Adventures action theme this week is to be thankful in everything." He wasn't thinking about her at all but rather his class of juveniles. From the little Kim had told Lisa it sounded interesting. "Tell me more." She matched her stride to his.

With a darting glance of faint surprise he complied. "It's one of the most fantastic experiences I've ever witnessed in changing behavior in a person. Not only do the students change, but with each course, I re-examine my own goals."

"You consider goals important then?" Lisa had discovered her goals seemed to vary from day to day depending on whom she'd been with last.

"Important!" The sound exploded from him. Abruptly he stopped, gripping her tennis bag and facing her. "The reason these kids are so lost is that they have no reason for living."

She stared at him wide-eyed.

He grimaced ruefully and began to walk again. "The great thing about the class is they discover a reason for living all on their own. When they finish the nine weeks, they know where they're going!"

Lisa wished she could be in this class. "That must be a good feeling." She sighed.

"Don't you know?"

"Of course," she lied, her chin immediately lifting. "But I don't go around acting as if I know it all." She knew it was a petty attack.

"I'm sorry if I've given that impression." Moving on again he didn't sound the least sorry. "I've learned the hard way the little I do know." Mark spaced each word. "And where to find the answers."

They stopped in the pathway confronting each other. Mark had a death grip on her tennis bag, his lids lowered so he could study her expression. She had her hands on her hips, her feet planted apart aggressively.

"And where's that?"

"The Bible."

The two words hung between them, silencing the desert sounds, reverberating around their little world.

Lisa was grateful for her concealing sunglasses, knowing she couldn't flippantly disagree. Since coming to live with her grandmother, she couldn't drag up any of the trite intellectual put-downs she had accepted in college. Frustrated and feeling childish, she stalked down the trail.

Her rapid movement startled the wildlife, and a brown lizard darted across her foot. Screeching, Lisa jumped backward. She nearly knocked Mark off balance, and he clutched at her. As a warm current surged through her limbs, Lisa pushed free. Laughing self-consciously, she tried to appear calm even though she knew the tiny freckles on her nose stood out from fright.

"Quick little monsters, aren't they?" Mark retrieved her bag and racket, giving her time to regain control. "The best way to enjoy the desert is on horseback. Do you ride?"

Taking one last steadying breath Lisa replied, "Not in ages."

Mark held back the hedge for Lisa to precede him into their yard. "We're here!"

Randal acknowledged their presence by waving his racket while he and Kim finished their kiss. Lisa didn't dare exchange a glance with Mark at this point. She walked directly to her position on the courts ready to warm up for the game.

Randal set the tone by saying, "Don't forget to protect your alley, Kim. And *move* when I holler!"

Unconsciously Lisa looked to Mark for his directions, then berated herself for appointing him leader of their effort. But when they lost the first game and Mark said, "Get back after the serve," she didn't rebel. She had sense enough to know cooperation was essential to winning.

Kim and Randal took the first set, their experience as tennis partners weighing to their advantage. But Mark and Lisa had learned how to gauge their opponents and managed to take the second set.

Before the third set Mark called to Randal, "Give us a minute. Lisa and I are going to discuss strategy." As if from a photographic memory he pointed out Randal and Kim's weaknesses and suggested ways to capitalize on them.

When Mark and Lisa won again, Kim accused her brother of using political maneuvers to win.

He laughed, "We had the psychological edge all along."

Pretending to pout Kim hung on Randal's arm and asked, "What do you mean?"

"We aren't preoccupied with love." Mark winked at Lisa.

Lisa's smile was automatic but, for some reason, she didn't think his statement humorous.

"Right now I'm preoccupied with something else." Randal rubbed his stomach and headed for the lunch basket.

Mark opened a container and sampled the savory taco salad. "How long do you get to stay this trip?"

"Until Sunday night. I have to go before dark." Randal munched a radish rosette and grimaced.

Kim shooed them out of the way and she and Lisa arranged the food on the bright red and yellow cloth on the grass. "I don't want him to be flying after the sun goes down. I worry about him anyway, crop dusting." She couldn't stop the catch in her voice. "So we'll make the most of his time. Tomorrow—"

"Tomorrow," interrupted Mark, "I thought you guys might like to ride over the place. Lisa rides."

"Great idea!" Eagerly Kim made plans. "Say we saddle up around two o'clock?"

"Fine." Randal smiled indulgently.

"I haven't been on a horse in four years," protested Lisa.

"You'll do fine," Kim assured her.

Lisa felt uneasy about the prospect of being with Mark again—or was it that she felt uneasy about his making plans to include her and assuming she'd go along? But she joined the continuing banter over barbecue, Mexican cornbread, salad, and fruit. As they were finishing Lisa thought of an excuse. "I need to work on my song." The moment she spoke Lisa regretted her words, for Mark's expression became alert.

"What song?"

No wonder he's a politician, thought Lisa. *He doesn't miss a thing.* "I'm singing Tuesday night on the local television talk show."

"Tuesday night!" Kim looked at Mark in astonishment. "Isn't that the night—" She never finished her sentence because Mark dropped several ice cubes down her back. Her squeals and jumping about sidetracked the question. Then Randal added to Kim's discomfort with some ice of his own. They began tussling, teasing, and chasing each other across the wide expanse of the lawn.

Mark stretched out on the grass and flung one hand over his forehead to shade his eyes. But Lisa could feel him watching her as she repacked the picnic hamper. She tried to ignore him, but every fiber of her body knew he was there, contemplating her.

"It's time for me to go." She tucked the last item in the hamper and closed the lid.

Mark rose to lean on his elbows as if to accompany her.

"I know the way." She needed to be alone, away from his overpowering presence. With an uneasy smile she added, "I enjoyed the tennis."

Returning to his reclining position Mark folded his arms beneath his head and looked at her intently. "Tomorrow at two, then, at the stables?"

She nodded, then stooped to go through the hedge. She hurried down the path until she was out of sight before she paused and took a deep breath. She felt as if she'd been holding it for a long time.

Calmer, she thought over the afternoon. They'd had fun, lots of fun. It had been pleasant and restful, at least until the very end when she had been left alone with Mark.

Lisa had been afraid the subject of the talk show would come up again. She was more worried than she liked to admit.

Because her grandmother would be watching, Lisa was having a terrible time deciding what to sing. She had always been so caught up in the rhythm and melody, she hadn't concerned herself much with a song's meaning. Now, she discovered herself picking each song apart, analyzing it for its message as well.

What made the difference? nagged an inner voice. *Coming to live with Grandmother*, Lisa answered. But the voice mocked, *Are you sure it wasn't meeting Mark London?*

She stopped in the path and shouted at the world, "No!"

Chapter Six

Is that really me? Lisa studied the picture in the Sunday edition of the newspaper. As always, there was an unreal quality about seeing herself in print.

In one picture, backed up by the four young men at drums, guitar, banjo, and piano from The Wind, Lisa looked the professional entertainer. She liked the other picture better. Ann Nix had taken it in her greenhouse retreat, plants abounding, and Lisa appeared to be practicing her autoharp. *It looks more natural, more...me,* Lisa concluded.

Lisa knew she could be sensational, the professional singer-entertainer in the other photograph, if she desired it. But the question always arose, did she want to?

That question had brought her to stay with Jewel. She slowly folded the newspaper and took a long look around the dew-drenched yard.

The ringing phone made Lisa realize she had stood too long contemplating the article in the early morning sun. Dropping the newspaper in Jewel's favorite chair, Lisa ran to answer.

"Lisa!" An exuberant male voice with a slight accent caressed her name. "Carl Valdez here. Before me is a fascinating newspaper spread. Congratulations! I knew you could sing, but this! Fantastic! May I have the honor of your company at lunch today?"

Why not have lunch with him? With someone enthusiastic about her singing, and an appreciative male at that?

"Thanks for asking. Don't forget we have church this morning." Even as she spoke she remembered that Dulce had Sundays off now. "Grandmother and I."

"Your grandmother is invited also." He didn't even hesitate, which made him rise in her estimation. "I could meet you there, perhaps?"

"Let me ask Jewel first." Lisa felt sure she would agree.

"Just warn him I must be home for my afternoon snooze by two." Jewel laughed, but they both knew she was serious because she needed the rest.

"Great. I'll be in front of the church then," Carl agreed.

When Lisa returned to the porch her grandmother was reading the article. "Very impressive." She indicated the half page of the society section devoted to Lisa.

Clearing her throat Jewel added, "Thank you for coming to me. You're a lovely girl, Lisa. Not only on the outside, but on the inside, too. No one else…cared enough." Her voice cracked.

Clasping Jewel's veined hands, Lisa knelt before her. "That's not true. You know they were just involved, and I wasn't. Actually," Lisa laughed, trying to lighten the mood, "I'm the selfish one. How could I pass up a live-in extended vacation for free?"

"You had this." Jewel pointed at the photograph of the singing group. "You planned to go on a summer tour. It says so right here."

"We thought about a tour. But I needed to stop, look,

and listen before I took a giant step in that direction. That's why I'm here, at the crossing." She abandoned her attempt at gaiety and put her head in Jewel's lap. "I don't know which way to take."

Jewel stroked the silky mass of curls. "What will the group do if you don't stay?"

"The drummer's girlfriend is dying to try." Waving a negligent hand, Lisa resettled her head in the security of Jewel's lap.

"She's good?"

"With practice she'll get better. Some of the guys object that she wouldn't be the same."

"You do have a magic aura about you when you sing," Jewel agreed.

"Yet the magic, the applause, the whole thing is such fleeting glory." Lisa found herself pointing out the pitfalls as if Jewel were encouraging her to go with the group. "So pointless. You see?" Lisa raised her eyes to meet Jewel's.

"I see."

After the morning church service Lisa was deluged with compliments and congratulations on the newspaper story. Laughing, her brown eyes sparkling and dimples flashing, Lisa promised everyone the opportunity to see and hear her on George Mahon's show Tuesday. Popularity and appreciation are transitory and fragile, but they are nice, Lisa decided.

A blanket invitation had been extended from the pulpit bidding everyone to come to the Londons' garden party, so a large circle of admirers surrounded Kim and Randal, too.

Kim, with Randal at her side, caught up with Lisa in the church foyer. "What are you planning to sing on George's show?"

"I'm not telling." Lisa smiled mysteriously. She wasn't about to admit she still hadn't decided.

Finally only Mark, Kim, Randal, Lisa, and Jewel remained. Mark hadn't commented on the newspaper article, and Lisa was miffed. Tilting her head and displaying a dimple she inquired, "And what do you think, Mr. London?"

"About the article?" His eyes glinting, he added, "or you?"

Color suffused her cheeks, and Lisa felt like kicking him. Too embarrassed to speak she turned and took a step away. Mark caught her arm. Instantly she froze, but she could not meet his eyes.

Sensing her withdrawal Mark dropped her arm as if it were a burning ember. "The article was interesting; and your photograph, lovely." He made certain everyone heard—an unspoken apology for teasing her.

Later, she thought, *later I'll think of something scathing to say*.

In a lower tone Mark spoke for her ears only. "Very lovely, Lisa. Forgive me, again."

"No...yes," she whispered, her head averted.

"Then if I'm forgiven, have lunch with me." Gently he caught her chin. "I'll take you by to change clothes before we ride at two."

"I can't, I'm sorry." *I really am sorry*, she realized as she smiled weakly and glanced through the glass front doors. "I have a date for lunch."

"Carl Valdez." Mark's eyes blazed with a yellow fire as he watched the black TransAm pull to the curb.

Smoothing his thick black hair, Carl came quickly up the church steps and took Lisa's hand. "I'm delayed. I hope you didn't wait long."

"Not long." Lisa pulled her hand free. "Grandmother is—" She pointed to the group across the foyer.

"I'll get her." Carl nodded curtly to Mark who only raised an eyebrow in acknowledgement.

While Carl assisted Jewel down the steps to his car, Mark demanded, "You will ride at two?"

She nodded and he left her. Slowly she followed the others.

"What's Mark London doing here?" Carl took his eyes from the road to glance at Lisa, this time beside him on the front seat.

She looked back at the church, but Mark wasn't visible.

From the back seat Jewel answered. "He plans to stay all summer. Some items he needed to attend to, he told me."

"All lousy summer!" Carl gripped the steering wheel as if to strangle it.

"I'm so glad." Unaware of Carl's suppressed anger, Jewel continued. "He needs to relax. Mark has too many irons in the fire."

"Doesn't he though!"

Immediately after Carl seated them in the Steakhouse Restaurant, he excused himself to make a phone call. Lisa studied the menu, then looked around. The decor had a Western flavor with wagon-wheel light fixtures. A large wagon in the center of the dining area served as a salad bar.

Carl seemed tense during the meal and unable to relax. When the meal came to an end he returned them promptly to the church to retrieve Jewel's car. Lisa was glad. Somehow Carl just wasn't on her wavelength.

After changing into jeans and a long-sleeve cotton shirt to protect her arms from the sun, Lisa settled Jewel for her afternoon nap. Then she fixed a glass of iced tea and picked up the morning newspaper again.

For a long time Lisa gazed at the picture of herself in the greenhouse, wondering at her own serene smile. Finally she studied the one of herself and the group with equal intensity. The vivacious young woman there seemed a person she had known an eon ago.

The article was well done, and her folks would want a copy. Since her grandmother had laid claim to this one, she should have picked up another paper in town. She would ask Kim for her copy.

Tying her long ash-blonde hair back with a wide ribbon, Lisa let herself out the back gate. She walked rapidly down the worn path to the Londons. When she arrived, Kim, Randal, and Mark had four horses saddled and ready to mount in the drive before the house.

Kim swung up on her roan, greeting Lisa with, "Good, you're here. Isn't it a gorgeous day!" She tested her stirrup length and gripped her reins while Randal swung up on his horse.

"By the way, could I have the clipping from your newspaper to send my folks?" Lisa knew Kim wanted to be alone with Randal, but it couldn't hurt to delay separating the party.

Kim steadied her horse. "That's the funniest thing. I was going to clip it myself, and our announcement picture, but I couldn't find the newspaper anywhere. Maybe Mother has it. Anyway, I'll be getting extra copies tomorrow and you can have some."

"Thanks." Lisa spoke both to Kim and to Mark, who handed her the reins to a pretty sorrel mare. He stood beside her while she mounted.

"Her name's Syrup." While Mark smoothed the mare's neck, she nuzzled him. Seeing Lisa safely on and confidently handling the reins, Mark swung up on a large appaloosa stallion sporting a bright blanket on his rump.

It felt good to be in the saddle again, but she knew she'd be sore later. When Kim shouted and took off in a gallop, Lisa followed with delight. She had forgotten how riding cleared her mind of everything except the horse, her body clinging close, and the wind rushing through her hair. It gave her a clean, exhilarated feeling—a simple joy in just being alive and pounding across the desert pastureland.

When she slowed, she realized Mark had been right behind her all the way, holding back his horse. Breathless, her face flushed, she exclaimed, "Great!"

Mark nodded. Following Kim and Randal, they walked their horses in companionable silence. Lisa soaked up the sun, not thinking, sometimes almost dozing. When they came to a draw and stopped, she realized more than an hour had passed comfortably, without an argument.

A large mesquite stood in the bottom of the arroyo, offering shade. Kim and Randal had already dismounted. Mark's tawny eyes twinkled. "I believe this is the refreshment center." He tipped his hat at the other couple.

When Lisa glanced over, all that was visible was the back of Randal's bent head. He was taking advantage of the stop to kiss Kim. Unthinking, Lisa smiled and turned back to Mark. When she met his mocking gleam, a blush washed her cheeks. Hastily she kicked her horse and trotted toward the lime-green mesquite, where she tied Syrup.

"I thought we were eating at the Homestead." Mark jumped down and dropped his reins.

"Oh, it'll be all dusty and dirty." Kim gave Randal another peck on his nose before moving to the saddlebag. "Let's eat here, and then ride on over there."

As Mark poured the iced tea into paper cups, Kim

took the assortment of carrot sticks, celery, and apples from the pouch. Randal groaned at this display. "No cake, no cookies? I'm starving, woman!"

Kim unwrapped the plastic wrap from the vegetables. "I've already bought my wedding dress. It's being altered to fit and I don't intend to gain a smidgin of weight!"

Grabbing a carrot stick, Randal munched it loudly, expressively.

"Look at you, Randal, submitting to this tyranny. That's a bad mistake," warned Mark, smiling wickedly.

"I know." Randal slumped his shoulders as if in submission. "But it's only for a little longer." He straightened up. "Until I have her irrevocably in my clutches. Then we'll see if I don't get cake!" He bared his teeth menacingly.

"Not if you don't stay sweet yourself!" laughed Kim. Dismissing the men and their foolishness she spoke to Lisa. "I've finally decided on my colors. We need to pick out the material for your dress."

Lisa picked up another slice of apple and savored the sweet juice. "What color?"

"When I saw you in that yellow jumpsuit I realized what a perfect color that would be for an August wedding. I want masses of yellow roses and white daisies."

"Sounds lovely." Lisa was pleased with the choice. She loved bright shades of lemon. "Have you decided on the songs?"

"You don't need to know yet, do you?"

"I just wondered." Why should there be any hurry about the wedding songs when she was still debating what to sing this Tuesday, two days away? She licked apple juice from her fingers before asking, "What are you wearing to the garden party? Long or short?"

"Long. I feel so utterly feminine in a long dress." Kim

81

swayed gently to give expression to her words.

Randal joined them. "I'll be glad when the party's over!"

Kim's mocking pout brought a smile as he explained, "Because when it's over you're coming home with me to visit my folks. Then I'll have you in the palm of my hand."

"Sounds fun!" Kim fluttered her lashes flirtatiously.

Feeling slightly uncomfortable with their oblivious love, Lisa finished her tea and moved to the horses. She restlessly mounted Syrup and rode down the gully. Topping a knoll she could see before her an old rambling ranch house. This must be the original homestead Mark spoke of with so much caring in his voice.

One portion of the house was of rough-cut lumber in the ship and lap style; another part was rock; the largest section, adobe. The yard around was hard-packed earth except for some mesquite and elm trees which long ago had been carefully watered to provide shade. Beyond the house were the outbuildings—a large barn of faded gray lumber and several smaller buildings and corrals.

Lisa's eyes returned to the house, her heart squeezing inside at the picture the homestead made with its split rail fence and the large, aging elms. She could almost picture the London ancestors struggling to make a home in this desolate land. Each addition to the house seemed a separate memorial to their courage.

Hearing the others coming up behind her, Lisa roughly dried her eyes with her cuff so they couldn't catch her with tears in her eyes. She was too sentimental to feel this surge of pride in being a part of this country and its heritage through her grandmother.

Kicking her mare to a trot, Lisa headed for the house. Suddenly she heard a cracking noise, and the dust rose in billows around Syrup's hooves. The horse shied, but

Lisa managed to hang on. She looked around for the cause.

Again there came a crack! Lisa gripped the reins firmly, frantically searching the ground for what must be a rattlesnake. The horse trembled violently and tried to get the bit in her teeth.

Her eyes on the ground, Lisa saw the bullet plow into the dirt and spray rocks on the horse's hooves. She didn't realize she had released some tension on the reins, but it was enough for the sorrel to lunge forward, tossing Lisa from the saddle.

Lisa lay stunned on the hot sand. She tried to get her brain together to move her body, but her head spun wildly. Bullets! She raised her head and tried to lift herself to a crawling position. Another shot made her collapse instinctively.

She closed her eyes trying to stop the tilting world and get a grip on herself. When she felt a hand on her arm she screamed, "No!" and rolled her body away into a tight curl.

"Lisa. It's me." Mark had snaked his way to her side.

Trying to blink the sand from her lids, she drew a deep breath and felt suddenly safer.

"Hang on." He quickly hoisted her over his shoulder and carried her in a zigzag crouching run back to the draw.

Shots blazed around them. Frozen with fear that each move would be Mark's last, Lisa dared not breathe during the whole run.

When they jumped down into the arroyo out of sight of the sharpshooter, Mark dropped her on the sand and collapsed beside her. Both gasped for air, and Lisa shuddered convulsively.

Mark gathered her in his arms and held her tightly.

Feeling safer, but still between hysteria and tears, Lisa opted for laughter.

Looking up at him through her lashes, she said, "I guess there are some advantages to being thrown."

Mark grinned and instead of pulling her to her feet picked her up again. He carried her farther down the gully where Kim waited.

Lisa realized her mind was still fuzzy, but she had the feeling she was taking part in an old Western movie. *We would be alone and the hero would seize this opportunity to kiss me.* "We're not alone," she murmured, a dreamy smile on her lips.

"But the temptation is almost irresistible." Mark breathed in her ear. Shivers ran through her body. Opening her eyes and wondering how much she had said aloud, she pushed back, tilting her head. "Syrup ran away."

"No problem. She's on her way home." Mark held her closer, so Lisa could feel the beating of his heart, a back-up bass to her own pulsing lead.

"I'm okay," she assured him, putting her hand on his chest and feeling the heat of his skin beneath the Western shirt.

Kim peered into her face. "You sure?"

"Positive." Lisa applied more pressure to free herself. Mark lowered her feet and helped her stand.

Looking at the knoll where they'd been, at Randal staring over the ridge trying to locate the gunman, Kim asked the question foremost in their minds. "Who's shooting?"

Mark gazed at the place on the horizon where the old house stood. "See anything?"

"Nope." Randal crawled down to join them. He untied their horses and helped Kim mount.

Rubbing his jawline thoughtfully, Mark narrowed his

eyes, then shrugged. "Probably kids, drinking or dop-ing." He pulled the reins of the appaloosa, who sidled toward him.

"Lisa can ride double with me," offered Kim, scoot-ing forward in her saddle.

"She rides with me." Mark grasped Lisa's waist and lifted her easily into the saddle. "Hands here, on the sad-dle horn," he instructed as he swung up behind her. Then he put his arm around her for support. Lisa shrank away in resistance as blood rushed through her veins at his touch. Feeling her withdrawal he held her closer. The battle of wills was a silent one. Lisa didn't want Kim or Randal to notice, so in the end, of course, Mark won.

At home later that afternoon, Lisa tried to push the in-cident from her mind. After Mark's easy explanation of the shooting, she didn't mention it to Jewel. Then Kim called.

"May I catch a ride with you to church tonight? Ran-dal has flown home, and Mark and the foreman have gone out to the old place to see what they can find."

"Of course." If Mark had returned to the old home-stead, then he wasn't so casual as he seemed about the shots.

"Thank you." Kim laughed pathetically. "I feel so lost without Randal. I didn't want to go to church alone."

Sitting between Kim and Jewel on the church pew that evening, Lisa heard little of the minister's sermon. The worry she felt for Mark's safety both surprised her and did strange things to her stomach. She kept having visions of blood and gunshots and Mark lying wounded or...dead.

Surely it had been just kids, nothing dangerous. But what if it hadn't been? Mark had made many enemies as a politician. She squirmed in her seat. Sitting through the sermon was so difficult. All she wanted to do was pray. Pray. *Take care of him, God; take care of him.* The words made a refrain in her head.

As they pulled up between the bell-laden gateposts at Jewel's, Kim suggested, "Why don't you come over and look at dress patterns, Lisa?"

"I'd love to!" Realizing Lisa had accepted without consulting her grandmother, Kim raised an inquiring eyebrow.

"I'll call if I need you." Jewel let herself in the door, pushing the dogs gently down from their eager welcome. "Honey and Goldie, of course, will be here with me."

"To be perfectly blunt," said Kim as they entered her room, "I didn't want to come home alone. Perhaps I'm extra touchy because Randal's gone, but everyone seems to be snapping at each other today." She flicked the switch at the door and a soft glow from indirect lighting above her canopy bed lit the room. She crossed the blue carpet and turned on a table lamp beside a small chintz-covered couch. On the table sat several pattern books. She patted the place beside her for Lisa.

"I think," Kim mused, picking up a book, "Flora is the instigator. She has been on a rampage, making us all tense. She's after Mark's hide especially. She snarls every time he appears. He'd fire her except for Mother and the garden party plans."

Lisa propped her feet on an ottoman and picked up another book.

"Inez jumps every time she's spoken to," Kim continued. "You met Inez, didn't you?"

Lisa nodded. "That day..."

"Oh, Dulce. That's right." Kim smile ruefully. "Anyway, I think Inez is worried about her nephew."

They turned the pages silently for a moment, but Lisa kept glancing out at the darkening sky.

Kim pointed out a pattern similar to the one she had selected for her wedding gown. An old-fashioned, high-necked style with lace and hundreds of tiny buttons down the back and on the sleeves, it would be very becoming to Kim.

Next they examined bridesmaids' dresses and both chose a similar high-necked style to be made in a yellow organza. Each bridesmaid would wear a large, white garden hat and carry white, yellow-centered daisies. As soloist, Lisa would have a circlet of daisies in her hair.

Lisa knew she should go home with the selections made, but she lingered in the hope of seeing Mark return safely home.

"How about some iced tea after all our big decisions?" Marking the place in the pattern book, Kim slammed it shut.

"Let me call Jewel first." Lisa gladly accepted Kim's offer. Jewel insisted she was fine and that Lisa was a worrywart.

As Lisa hung up the phone, Kim crouched in a stealthy position and whispered, "Remember Flora—so tippy toe." She crossed the room in this fashion, straightening up at the door. In a more normal tone she said, "Actually, she should be gone by now, but she doesn't like anything touched in her kitchen, so we'll have to be careful not to leave a trail."

Fortunately Flora had retired to her apartment over the garage. Feeling like burglars, they dug through the cabinets and drawers trying to decide what to eat. Lisa had her back to the kitchen door when Mark stepped in.

"Good evening, ladies."

Her heart lurched at the sound of his voice. She dropped the bag of Fritos and turned, her hand at her throat. "You startled me." He was okay!

Lisa knew it couldn't have been even a few seconds, but his eyes held hers, somehow reassuring her. He knew she had been worried for his safety.

Then, surveying the room, Mark rubbed his hands together in glee. "Food! Can I have some?"

"Any suggestions or additions?" As she carried cheese, lettuce, and tomatoes to the table, Kim said, "We were hauling this feast to my room, but with Flora out maybe we can get away with eating it here."

Sorting through the canned goods cabinet, Mark plaintively inquired, "Did we have supper? I can't remember it."

"Right, we didn't." Kim added paper plates to the pile on the table. "We never do on Sunday evening so Flora can be off. But she was in and out all day, and that thing—" Kim frowned at the CB base station, "was going continually."

Mark pulled out a can. "Chili! Over Fritos and cheese, and topped with lettuce and tomatoes." He licked his lips.

"Sounds delicious."

While they ate Kim demanded a report on Mark's investigations.

"We found empty beer cans, cigarette butts, and empty shells." He took another bite. "Probably some kids drinking and target practicing. Always a problem with an abandoned place."

Accepting his casual dismissal of the shooting, Kim turned to Lisa. "What song are you going to sing on the talk show?"

"I haven't decided, exactly. I have to work on it tomorrow."

"But you'll have time for a quick tennis game, won't you?" Kim looked guiltily at the plate before her and shoved it away. "I must stay in shape for the wedding...and everything."

Mark laughed outright as Kim blushed and Lisa wished she were home. Earlier she would have died rather than leave until Mark returned; now she wanted more than anything to be gone. She picked up her glass and paper plate.

"I need to get back to Jewel."

"But you called and told her you were staying."

"I don't like her to be alone this late since the prowler incident. And I'm walking, which will take a bit."

Mark stacked his plate on Kim's and tossed them in the garbage. "I'll walk you home."

"Thanks, but it's plenty bright enough to see."

Mark ignored her objections and moved with her out the door and across the lawn. But he seemed preoccupied as they walked the now-familiar path in the moonlight. Lisa felt tongue-tied, so the walk to The Bells was silent.

Lisa couldn't sleep for reliving the walk. All the way she had been intensely aware of Mark beside her. He was not just a tall, self-assured man. Mark was a man she respected because he had thought seriously about what he was doing and where his life was going. But more than that, Lisa couldn't forget the strength of his hand on her arm or the warmth of his embrace when he had pulled her to safety.

In the darkness that night she stood at her window watching the play of light and shadow from the moon. Mark London was a man who knew where he was going. *Do I know where I'm going?* she asked herself. *No*, came the answer. But now she knew what she would sing on Tuesday, the theme from *Mahogany*, "Do You Know?" Lisa could sing it with empathy. She thought surely now she could sleep, but still she sat on the window seat.

"There's the moon, a reflection of the sun, proving the sun is still around." She blinked her eyes in surprise. "That's it!"

The words exactly fit the tune that plagued her mind. She repeated the words, adding to, changing—sleep forgotten as the second verse of the song she was composing became concrete.

But several hours later when she finally slept, the refrain in her mind was from *Mahogany*. "Do you know where you're going to?"

Chapter Seven

Through the intercom speaker in the waiting room, Lisa could hear George Mahon, the host of the talk show, leading up to her introduction. Nervously she studied her reflection in the full-length mirror. The long kelly-green dress swirled around her feet and emphasized her ash blonde hair.

But only vaguely did she register the perfection of her appearance. She was recalling the events surrounding her arrival at the studio.

That afternoon while she was in the greenhouse practicing, Mark had come over to see Jewel. He hoped she would hire a young man from his class to get the garden and yard in shape.

Jewel and Mark had decided something else as well. By some strange coincidence Mark was to appear on the same talk show as Lisa, to publicize a fund-raising rodeo benefiting juvenile delinquents. Without asking Lisa, they decided that Mark would bring Kim over to view the program with Jewel and then take Lisa to the station with him. When Lisa, fire in her eyes, questioned Jewel, her grandmother resorted to fluttery handwavings.

It was the same old thing—Mark making arrangements for her without asking. Not that Lisa didn't feel a certain warm spot in her heart that he wanted her with him, but he could have asked *her*.

The voice coming over the speaker now was Mark's. He was already on stage discussing the rodeo. Naturally the interview had also covered why he was encouraging his constituents to support state-owned liquor licenses.

And now George Mahon announced her name. The curtains parted and Lisa stood in the spotlight. She was suddenly overcome with stage fright, as if she had never sung in public! Why this onslaught of butterflies?

Trying to regain her calm Lisa walked to the host, smiled blindly at him, and knew she was going to have to grope for a chair if someone didn't help her quickly!

In the overwhelming brightness her eyes weren't focusing. The butterflies had left her stomach and lodged in her throat. Turning and extending her hand toward some furniture, she felt Mark grip her hand and guide her down to the chair. Gratefully Lisa smiled into his hazel eyes.

And right there in front of the host and his television audience, Mark slowly smiled in return. Lisa felt a warmth even greater than that from the lights. The reassuring squeeze he gave her hand as he released it brought courage surging back. Turning to the host she easily fielded his first question. Suddenly she felt brilliant, witty, on top of the world. When it was time for her number, she was ready.

As a hush fell over the audience she softly began the haunting melody—"Do you know where you're going to?" She sang it from the depth of her own inner turmoil. Forgetting the audience, the host, even Mark, she asked this question of the world.

When Lisa finished there was a breathless silence while the audience awoke from their dream. Then applause resounded, echoing through the barn-like studio. Cries were raised for more. "Encore, encore!"

George Mahon was on his feet, coming across the stage to second their enthusiasm. "One more. Please do just one more. If I had only known—"

"I haven't rehearsed anything. I don't think—surely, your time schedule?"

Mark stood beside her now, his face bright, his hand warm, supporting her arm. "Perhaps one of your grandmother's favorites. One you've sung for her?"

Another lifeline extended. "I could sing 'Amazing Grace.' But do you think I should?" Instinctively she consulted Mark.

"You should." With a barely perceptible caress of her arm, he accompanied the host back to their places.

So Lisa sang "Amazing Grace," glad she could do that special something for her grandmother. Then rather than return to the chairs by the host, she bowed and left through the draperies. From experience she had learned it was better to leave the audience wanting more.

In the waiting room once again she could hear the compliments and, of course, it was thrilling. Carefully she listened, hoping to catch Mark's voice added to the praise, but she never did.

Finally the program ended. Minutes passed and Mark still didn't arrive. Had he forgotten her? What was he doing? Determined she wouldn't seek him out, she meticulously repaired any damage to her makeup. She restored some of the curls piled high on her head, smoothed a kiss curl near her ear, and became more and more agitated. Just when she thought he might have left, he opened the door.

"I'm sorry. We were in a technical discussion and it was difficult to get away." Picking up the ivory lace shawl her grandmother had insisted she bring, he placed it gently around her shoulders.

The shawl felt good because suddenly she was very cold inside. When his lean fingers caressed her shoulders she almost jumped from the warmth which swept through her body. Swiveling her body around to face him and tilting her chin with a firm hand, Mark said, "You're good, Lisa. Very good."

The ultimate accolade, thought Lisa. Her dimple responded as Lisa smiled, curtsying slightly so she could move away from his magnetic presence. "Thank you, kind sir."

"I feel like a cup of coffee. How about you?"

"I'm famished!"

"You didn't eat before the program?" He raised a brown eyebrow.

"Sherlock!" Pertly she cocked her head. Then, more seriously, "I couldn't. Surely you un—"

"I'm glad you couldn't. Now we can celebrate your success over dinner."

Breathlessly she agreed, wondering if this heady feeling came from the crowd's acclaim or his nearness.

While they waited to be seated in the foyer of the Sea and Sail Restaurant, a remodeled Victorian house, Lisa had a moment to reflect. It was marvelous for once to look as ravishing as possible, to know you've just been a smash hit, and to be escorted by a ruggedly handsome man.

The young hostess, dressed in Victorian costume, led them to a secluded corner table with an excellent view. The owner had gone to great pains to decorate with Victoriana, giving an atmosphere of graceful elegance.

"This is okay, Mr. Mark?" The young woman looked anxious.

"Fine, Becky. How's your mother?" He was obviously interested.

"Much better now!" She beamed, filled their water glasses, and opened the menus. "You need anything, you let me know." She bustled away.

Lisa concentrated on the menu, trying not to be curious about their hostess.

"Becky's a graduate of one of my Adventures classes." Mark glanced appraisingly around the restaurant. "This looks like a pleasant place to work."

Lisa agreed, glad for the opening he'd given her to ask about his classes. "Tell me more about this program. How many classes have you conducted?"

"I think I'm on my sixth class."

He seemed diffident, which surprised her considerably. Mark London—diffident? Finally she asked another question. "What are the meetings like? What happens?"

"They're great!" Fiercely Mark said this, then grinned sheepishly. "But if I get started on this subject there's no stopping me. Have you made your selection?" It was an effective change of subject, for Lisa became aware of Becky watching them.

"You choose." She folded her menu. "I prefer iced tea."

Sampling the creamy dressing on her salad, Lisa approached the subject again. "I really want to know about your classes." A dimple flashed. "I don't care if you do get wound up."

Impulsively Mark caught her hand as she reached for her water glass. "You're sure?" She lifted the glass and pulled her hand free but nodded.

Then he slowly grinned and threatened, "You asked for it. But I'll try to give you a capsule report. Adventures in Living Free is a personal development course. Each session is designed around class participation. I

95

have no personal input; I simply follow the manual. Assistants carry on the paper work, and we take a deep breath and dive in for nine weeks."

"It sounds amazingly simple." Lisa couldn't believe this was all there was to it, after the things she'd heard and seen, considering Dulce and now Becky. "How can you account for its acceptance and astounding results?"

"I must confess some participants never come around. And," Mark grimly shook his head, "the first few sessions are so hostile you could cut the air with a knife. Sometimes that is tried, too."

The picture this conjured up did nothing for Lisa's peace of mind.

"But the percentages are better with this program than any other I've tried."

"You've tried others, then?" How long had he been doing this—working his heart out over these kids?

"Too many before I stumbled onto this, but it's easy to bypass the simple approach as worthless."

Then Lisa asked the question she had been thinking of all evening, "Why? Why do you do this? Why are you so concerned with these kids?"

Again she felt Mark's eyes searching hers before he answered, demanding something she wasn't sure she could give.

"Lisa." His voice caressed her name. "I'd like to tell you. I've been wanting to." He paused as if formulating his words. But Becky appeared with platters of fish, so he remained silent. When she left, he started to speak again, but a high-pitched voice called his name.

A sultry, silver-streaked brunette in a long silver lamé dress led a party of people to their table. "Mark, we caught you on George's show. Although your portion was overshadowed by that singer. She—"

Abruptly Mark rose and interrupted, "Sheila. I'd like

96

you to meet Lisa Beall." Smoothly he gestured toward Lisa.

Putting down her fork Lisa looked at the woman, noting her obvious beauty and her possession of Mark's arm. She also saw a vulnerable quality in the blue eyes as her gaze left Mark to smile politely at Lisa.

"Lisa, this is Sheila Richardson-Baird."

Sheila studied Lisa as if discovering some repulsive lab specimen. "You're the singer!" If Lisa hadn't caught that vulnerable look earlier she would have been alarmed by the hardness in Sheila's eyes. "We saw the show."

Lisa nodded briefly and realized Sheila was avoiding any complimentary remark about her performance.

Soon all the others moved on to the reserved table except one man and Sheila. From their conversation Lisa gathered he owned a liquor store and wanted to question Mark about his new bill. While they talked Sheila turned back to Lisa. "You're good." The phrase now wounded like an insult. "What are you doing *here*?"

Lisa couldn't misunderstand Sheila's question. It implied that Lisa was good enough to be touring, so why was she wasting her time in a backwater like Three Rocks? In a way it was a backhanded compliment. "I'm staying with my grandmother, Jewel Beall."

"Oh yes, you did mention that." Lowering her voice Sheila added, "Not a long stay, I trust? Three Rocks is bound to be disappointing." Pointedly she looked toward Mark.

"Oh?" Lisa turned white at Sheila's obvious insinuation. Her instinct was to pick up the challenge and fling it at her. She dug her nails into her palms. She had no intention of marrying Mark London. They were as far apart as the two poles. Sheila could have him.

97

But Sheila had more to say. "—and isn't Mark's devotion to his delinquents remarkable?" Once again Lisa caught the conniving look in Sheila's cold blue eyes. "Of course you know why—" She suspended her sentence as Mark turned to them. Smiling brightly Sheila said, "It's been nice." She placed her hand on Mark's arm. "I'm looking forward to the engagement party."

When Mark reclaimed his seat he noticed that Lisa was pale. "Is something wrong?"

"I'm tired." Lisa knew it would be useless to say she was fine. Mark was too observant so she might as well be as honest as possible. She *was* angry and tired. Suddenly Lisa felt exhausted, as if her last resource had been depleted.

Mark offered to leave but she insisted they finish their meal, and managed to eat enough to satisfy him. They talked, but the conversation wasn't free and easy anymore.

His jaw taut, Mark allowed her to retreat into silence all the way home. But when she stepped from the car after he opened her door, he didn't move aside. Instead he demanded, "What's wrong, Lisa? I thought finally we were communicating. Then—bang! You withdrew."

Raking an agitated hand through his thick brown hair, he sighed, "For the life of me, I can't think what it could be. What did I do?" Taking her shoulders he rotated her so the porchlight illuminated her face, trying to discern some clue from her fixed expression.

Lisa twisted away. "I'm exhausted. Isn't that enough?" She started up the stone path.

Striding after her, Mark seized her arm. "It isn't enough! I want more—" Fiercely he jerked her into his arms and kissed her. Lisa tried to pull free, but her efforts were futile against his superior strength. She knew she couldn't escape. She had not been able to when he had nearly run her down, then shaken her into submission. Now his lips were claiming submission of another kind, making her forget to struggle, evoking her eager response. Then suddenly she was loose, stumbling backward.

Mark shoved his hands in his pockets and studied her. "I should apologize, but I'm not going to. I've apologized to you for the last time." Stalking to the door of the Monte Carlo, he got in and drove off, slowly.

Lisa realized then that Mark London never gunned a car engine, not even in anger.

Kim met Lisa at the door. "Oh, is Mark gone? I hoped to catch a ride with him." She closed the screen door. "Lisa, you were wonderful on the show!" Then she realized that Lisa was tensely silent. "But I know you're tired. I'll just run on home."

Without a word Lisa watched her go. Putting on a determined smile, she stepped inside to greet Jewel.

"Lisa!" The older woman rose from her chair and held out her arms. As Lisa stumbled into their enfolding security she knelt and let the tears fall freely. Just to be there, held tightly in her grandmother's comforting arms, was solace. When the tears finally ceased she sniffed, wiped at her smeared mascara, and managed a weak laugh. "I'm tired."

"I see that." Jewel nodded sympathetically, offering her ever-handy, white, lace-trimmed handkerchief. "Performing must be a dreadful strain on a person. But you're good, Lisa. Very good."

Mark had said that. Then Sheila had made the phrase an affront. Now her grandmother gave the words significance and dignity. "You're good, Lisa. Very good."

As she contemplated the moon from her window just before slipping into bed, Lisa asked with cynical introspection, *Good—but good for what?*

Chapter Eight

Kim tucked the tennis balls in the can and snapped on the plastic lid. "That's it. Six-four, seven-six. You weren't concentrating today, Lisa."

Restlessly Lisa swung her racket at a fly. "I know."

"I'm on my way to town. Want to come?"

"I've tons to do." It was an exaggeration since Dulce had taken over, and Lisa regretted her refusal the minute Kim left her at her grandmother's gate and drove off.

The tennis game had keyed her up and she felt unusually restless as she changed in her room with its fading wallpaper. The faded climbing roses on the paper only reminded her that time marches on, leaving frail humanity to do what it will. Quickly abandoning her room she headed for the tool shed.

Jewel called to her from the back porch. "What are you up to?"

"Pulling weeds." *That ought to work off this restless feeling.*

"Don't forget Mark is bringing José today to start working in the yard." Jewel waved her washcloth and stepped back inside.

"Rats!" Lisa kicked at a dandelion. She certainly didn't want to be here in the yard when Mark arrived.

So she decided to work on one of her songs instead.

From her greenhouse hideaway, Lisa saw Mark enter the back yard with Jewel and José. While Jewel pointed out the jobs to be done, Lisa tried to study the young Hispanic with Mark. About nineteen, he was brown-skinned and slim.

But her eyes kept rebounding to Mark, clad today in Levi's, boots, a long-sleeved Western shirt rolled up on muscled arms, and an old Stetson shading his eyes. The work clothes seemed as much a part of his personality as the casually natty suits he wore, or even his tennis whites. This knowledge irritated Lisa, and she gave up composing music for the day.

The days passed, each hotter and more depressing than the last. Lisa played tennis with Kim, listened patiently to her plans for her wedding and after, and tried to be interested when she raved about Randal's virtues. A week vanished. It was Wednesday again.

After church services that evening Lisa hastened Jewel to the car, not wanting to linger in the foyer. Kim waylaid her.

"Lisa, wait. I want to talk to you." Mark was going out to the car, and Kim called to him, "I'll only be a minute." Clutching Lisa's arm dramatically, Kim exclaimed, "Lisa, you have to come early and stay the whole time at the garden party! Suddenly I'm nervous and—" She blinked firmly. "Say you'll come and stay the whole time."

"You'll have Randal." Lisa felt she couldn't submit herself to the torture of Mark's antagonistic silence for a whole afternoon.

"It's not the same. I need you. Please, Lisa. I..." she faltered. "Suddenly the whole thing is getting too big for me." Her grip tightened and Lisa felt Kim tremble.

Berating herself for being so weak-willed, Lisa sighed in defeat. "What time?"

"Come at ten and stay until four." Kim's relief was obvious.

"Jewel planned to make only a quick appearance."

"Mark can go get her. Or no, bring her with you. You can run her home, then come back. What are you wearing?"

Mentally examining her closet, Lisa couldn't think of anything she would ever want to wear. "Didn't you say you were wearing something long?"

"A light green organza blouse and long printed skirt. It's not too dressy, but with a corsage it should be practical for the siege." Kim's irrepressible exuberance had already overcome her earlier fears.

"The green will make your hazel eyes turn that color."

As she noticed Mark's restless pacing, Kim squeezed Lisa's arm in appreciation. "I must go. Mark will be patient only so long."

At home, after helping Jewel to her room, Lisa went straight to her closet and flung open the door. What could she wear? Why hadn't she thought of this earlier instead of moping around? She flipped through her dresses rejecting each. She had to have something new.

Decisively she rushed down the hall to Jewel's room where a light still glowed beneath the door. Tapping lightly Lisa called, "Jewel?" Realizing what she had done, she changed it. "Grandmother?"

"Come in, come in."

Lisa opened the door timidly.

"Do call me Jewel, if you feel natural doing it. I've always liked my name." Her eyes twinkled kindly.

"It did come out naturally. If you don't mind…"

With an inviting pat on the side of her bed, Jewel

made room for Lisa. "Now what may I help you with?"

"I've got to have a new dress for tomorrow." Lisa flushed at Jewel's speculative look but continued with determination, "And you must help me choose one."

Jewel's eyes brightened in anticipation. "Rather short notice, isn't it?"

Suddenly feeling sheepish, Lisa smiled. "I know. But I must have a new dress."

"What about the one you wore for the show?"

"Too dressy, and Kim's wearing green." Lisa slid off the bed and wandered to the window, playing with the fringe on the rose-colored tieback. "I need to feel...right."

Lisa returned to the bedside. Jewel tenderly brought Lisa's hand to her cheek, stroking it. "It's very important to feel right, always."

"So," Lisa shared a conspiratorial smile with Jewel and they giggled like two girls. "I *need* a new dress!"

The next afternoon, Lisa settled Jewel in a rattan chair on the Londons' patio. "Will this do?" She shifted the chair slightly so the afternoon sun didn't shine directly on the older woman.

"I'm fine, Lisa." Jewel tucked her purse in her lap and took out the white lace handkerchief. "Go encourage Kim. She looked like a lost puppy when we came through the gate. I'm sure with the engagement party actually under way, she's petrified at the reality."

Even after this suggestion Lisa fussed over Jewel. "Would you care for punch now?"

"Not yet. There's Fern." Jewel spied a friend her age and waved. "Run along, dear."

Watching Fern approach, Lisa still clung to her grandmother's side. She dreaded the ordeal of joining Kim, Randal, Mrs. London, and most of all, Mark, at the gate.

Just before Fern reached them, Jewel whispered,

"Doesn't the dress feel right, Lisa?"

Lisa looked down, spreading the three-quarter length black cotton peasant skirt, border-printed with pink and red flowers. The white gypsy blouse draped with the organdy shawl of matching border print accented the blonde tints in her hair. The salesclerk had suggested the red silk flower perched above her right ear.

"Lisa?" Jewel repeated her name, demanding a reason for Lisa's hesitation.

Deciding to face Mark rather than go into explanations with her grandmother, Lisa smiled brilliantly and left. So many people were arriving at the gate that introductions and escorting the different groups to the refreshment tables made private conversations impossible. An hour quickly passed. Then Fern attracted Lisa's attention during a slight lull.

Lisa went to Jewel's side. "Are you ready to leave?"

Jewel patted her hand. "Fern and I have a bit more visiting to do, so she's going to take me home. This way we'll miss the four o'clock rush." Lisa helped Jewel down the steps and strolled with them toward Fern's car. Jewel admonished, "You should get something to drink and catch a quick breath yourself."

Returning to the yard, Lisa saw that Randal had taken Kim off to one of the white, wrought iron garden chairs in a shady spot near the gate. Mark was handing Sheila Richardson-Baird a crystal cup of punch. Lisa decided at once to take Jewel's advice.

She checked the gate once more to be certain she wasn't needed. Carl Valdez was just entering. He headed straight for Lisa. She smiled at him like a long lost friend.

"Carl, how nice!"

"Very nice." His brown eyes glittered, including everything in one gesture: the party arrangements, her

104

beauty, and her desirability.

His blatant appreciation was a balm to her wounded spirit, so she accepted his offer to get punch and refreshments. Choosing a hanging basket-chair beneath a large elm, Lisa arranged her skirt and gazed around at the magnificently decorated yard while Carl went to the nearest food table.

Mrs. London hadn't considered the cost, doing her best to eclipse any previous engagement party in the area. Canopied tables arranged in a circle gave a gazebo effect and were filled with delicious food. Garlands of daisies were draped all around. Groupings of white wrought iron furniture were scattered about for congenial visiting among the guests, and white wicker swings hung from the trees. Flowers abounded, centering the small tables and overflowing on the buffet tables, entwining the supporting poles and wires. Waiters rushed about collecting and refilling cups, passing food and drink with abandon. When an occasional lull came in the general noise, soft music floated across the lawn.

"Fruit punch." Carl handed her the cup and saucer and waved at the tray a waiter held. "I have brought an assortment."

Lisa realized she'd been in such a dither about getting her hair washed and dried after a morning of shopping she hadn't taken time for lunch. Selecting a petit four she indicated a metal chair near her swing. "Sit there, why don't you?"

"Big show." The curl to Carl's lip expressed his sentiments more exactly. "Cost tons, but Mark London has it." Swiftly Carl downed his punch and set the cup aside. "I see Mark's still in town." He nodded toward Mark and Sheila still chatting beneath a shade tree.

Glancing at them beneath her lashes Lisa took a bite of sandwich and mumbled a response.

"Who's that with him?" Carl appraised the shapely brunette holding Mark captive. "She looks familiar."

"Sheila Richardson-Baird." To say the name made Lisa feel a knot in her stomach.

Slowly Carl repeated the name. "Of course, those two—together!" Through lowered lids Carl broodingly watched the couple.

Unable to eat all the food after all, Lisa placed her cup and saucer on the little table between them. Her movement brought Carl out of his trance. "Mark London!" He growled the name.

Lisa raised an eyebrow at his expletive. "Why the heat?"

"You don't know?" Astonished, Carl raised his head to study her face. "You really don't know! You've been here almost a month and you really, truly don't have any idea?" From the puzzled expression in her clear brown eyes her sincerity was obvious.

"Well, well." A bitter smile twisted his smoothly handsome face. "But why should I be surprised? Money can cover anything. And, of course, Mark London is such a reformed character that we shouldn't mention something out of the dirty past, should we?" Carl smirked. "Hah! Money hides a multitude of sins!"

"Carl, really! He's your host."

"He also—" Carl stood abruptly, almost knocking over the chair. Grimly he continued, enunciating each syllable as if a lesson learned by rote, "Twelve years ago he also killed my wife."

I'm not here, Lisa thought wildly. Her hands gripped the sides of the wicker swing until her knuckles whitened. She knew she couldn't still be in the garden because all around her was blackness and in its midst a neon sign flashed off and on: *Killed my wife. Killed my wife*!

When the sign began to fade to gray and the sun registered in her sight again, when a breath finally shuddered from her body, Lisa still could not believe Carl's words.

"And now for the gory details." Carl had picked up his cup and swirled the dregs as he talked.

"No." The word was a faint sound Carl couldn't hear.

"We were having a party...a little fun, and Roberta, she was beautiful—beautiful—" He choked over a lump in his throat, before adding, "and too smart. We had a few drinks—"

Lisa forced herself to stand, to leave, she didn't want to hear—

Suddenly José, the young man Mark had brought to work in Jewel's yard, ran into the garden. Frantically he looked around until he spotted Mark and rushed to him.

At this interruption Carlos forgot his story and rose. "José! What's he doing here?"

Lisa could only shake her head at his question. She was relieved that something, anything, had terminated Carl's story. As if in a stupor she watched José gesture and talk. Then Mark put his arm around the young man and escorted him out the gate to the garage.

"What's he doing here?" Carl's eyes narrowed as he watched Mark and José leave.

"José?" Lisa tried to concentrate on Carl's new topic. "José was helping here before the party, placing chairs, carting trash, and doing last-minute chores." She remembered then that a few minutes before the guests began to arrive Mark had given José some refreshments and sent him back to The Bells. Jewel had just left the garden party with Fern a few minutes ago! Was something wrong with her? "José!"

Carl looked exasperated. "Yes, what's he doing with

Mark?" Without answering she started to follow the two, but Carl gripped her arm. "How does José know Mark?"

The pain was bruising but it brought Lisa out of her daze. "He's in Mark's class. Now, let me go." She raised her chin and pulled free.

But Carl was unaware of her. His eyes had taken on a faraway expression. "Of course." His words had no audience.

Lisa dashed to the back of the yard and through the gap in the hedge. With her car blocked in, it would be faster to run to The Bells. Of course, it might be all for nothing, but she had to be positive. Lisa didn't think she could bear it if something happened to Jewel.

Within ten minutes she breathlessly entered the back gate and ran through the kitchen to the living room. There she stopped, cheeks flushed, chest heaving, and took in the tableau before her.

Jewel and Fern looked on while Mark and José attended to Dulce, stretched out on the couch. Jewel handed Mark an afghan which he used to cover the girl.

As Mark settled back on his haunches, Lisa asked, "What happened?"

Jewel moved to Lisa's side. "Dulce was attacked."

"Attacked?"

"It's awful!" Jewel's grip on Lisa's hand tightened. "José discovered her and surprised the man. He escaped when José paused to check on Dulce. If only I hadn't locked Goldie and Honey in the dog run—"

"He dropped your portable television on the front lawn." Mark's eyes flicked quickly over Lisa before returning to Dulce.

"When I saw the TV dumped on the front lawn I insisted we shouldn't enter the house." Fern nodded at Mark. "Then they drove up."

Putting a supporting arm around Jewel, Lisa stepped closer to the couch. "Is she badly hurt?" José looked sick with anguish as he knelt and fidgeted beside Dulce.

"A big knot on the back of her head." Mark gently probed through her hair. "I can't find anything else. She may have a slight concussion—" He quit speaking as Dulce stirred.

Flickering her eyelids Dulce stared at the faces around her. As she spoke Jewel and Lisa moved to her side.

"*Señora* Beall, *mi Señora*. I'm so sorry…the man, thief…I heard a noise, then turn…" She closed her eyes tightly, remembering the blow. "I'm sorry."

Jewel smoothed Dulce's brow with her cool hand, forcing Mark to shift out of her way. "As long as you're not seriously hurt, everything's okay. Don't worry about it, dear. Just rest. I'll be right here." Gratefully Jewel dropped on the ottoman Mark tucked beneath her.

Fern regretfully said, "I guess I should be going now."

"Thank you for bringing Jewel home." Lisa escorted Fern to the door. "It does seem as if everything is under control now."

For a moment Lisa stood watching Fern depart, trying to sort through the events of the afternoon, an afternoon not yet over. Instantly Carl's cruel, bitter words began to resound in her head. She tried to shut them out when she returned to the living room.

Mark was questioning José. "What made you come inside? You were working in the yard."

"*Si*." José hung his head, his eyes avoiding Mark's. Now that Dulce had revived, he wasn't cooperating.

"Then why did you come inside?"

"I heard a cry, a groan—" José's dark eyes slid to Dulce. "I called, but no answer, only the dogs barking, so I come see." For a moment his chin raised and his eyes challenged Mark. Then clamping his lips shut José waited to see which way Mark's interrogation would go, not willing to say anything more.

"And what did you see?" Indicating a chair near the couch for José, Mark leaned back in an arm chair. But José ignored this offer, remaining beside the couch.

"I saw a man running across the porch and Dulce on the floor. I stopped to make sure she was alive." Again he cast his eyes at Dulce, awake though dazed, who watched him. "I ran after the...man and called. He dropped the TV." José shrugged in a Latin gesture indicating the end of his tale.

"Did you get a look at his face?" Mark's amber gaze and intense look pleaded for honesty. "Do you think you could describe him?"

José swallowed. Finally with a deep breath he lowered his head to study the brown shag carpet at his feet. "No." More firmly, "No!"

Lisa, listening intently to every inflection, knew José was lying. Mark's jaw flexed grimly in resignation, but he said nothing, only glancing at Dulce whose lids swiftly closed.

Standing and thrusting his hands in his pockets Mark said, "I suppose our robber figured everyone would be at the garden party, not knowing about Dulce or you, José?"

José only blinked and shrugged again, accepting whatever Mark wanted to surmise. Nodding at Dulce, Mark took Jewel's hand.

"Dulce will be fine with some rest. I'll arrange with her family for her to stay tonight. I'll have Dr. Nelson drop by on his way home from the engagement party."

"Fine." Jewel gladly accepted Mark's control of the situation. "José and I can handle everything now."

For a second Mark studied José who had moved protectively nearer Dulce.

"Lisa should return with you." Jewel's usually merry eyes were strained. She reminded her granddaughter, "Kim is counting on you."

"I—" Meeting Mark's cold expression Lisa ceased her stuttering and clenched her fists in the folds of her skirt. "I'm ready." She trailed him to his car.

Mark drove in silence. Lisa stared out the window, never looking at him, knowing if she spoke her voice would betray her by breaking with emotion, and then the tears would flow. And what could she say—*I know your secret?* Never.

How she lived through the rest of the party Lisa didn't know. Carl tried to corner her, but finally he gave up and left.

As she helped speed the last guests to their cars, her smile felt as if it were cracking at the corners. Keeping firm control of herself Lisa even managed to encourage Kim while she changed. She and Randal were flying to visit her future mother-in-law's home for two weeks.

Nervously Kim paced her blue carpet. "I've met her, of course—and like her." She rearranged her clothing in her suitcase. "But it won't be the same."

"You'll have a lovely time." Lisa tried to keep her mind on Kim's anxiety, instead of demanding Kim's version of the bizarre story Carl had begun. "You'll probably discover you two have tons of things in common besides doting on Randal. They've planned a shower and a get-acquainted party for his friends to meet you. You'll be rushed off your feet."

"All true." Kim grinned ruefully and closed the suitcase. "But that doesn't keep me from being frightened." Catching a glimpse of her tragic face in the mirror, Kim pretended to tremble and then laughed to defy her fear.

111

"You'll do." Lisa joined Kim before the mirror and hugged her tightly. "I'm glad you're my friend." Sudden tears dimmed her brown eyes.

Returning the embrace and stepping back with a determined business-like attitude, Kim noticed Lisa's tears. "You're crying!"

"Silly me." Lisa smiled through the tears but she was unable to stop them. Wiping ineffectively at the continuing flow, Lisa picked up the suitcase and shoved the nightcase at Kim. "You're ready now, aren't you?"

Thinking Lisa was crying for her, Kim straightened her spine and tried to reassure her. "I'll be fine, Lisa."

"Then I'll say good-bye now instead of coming out to the airstrip," Giving Kim another squeeze before sniffing valiantly, Lisa watched her friend skip down the stairs. "Have a good time, Kim."

Then Lisa slipped down the backstairs and around to her car. Tears continued to blur her vision as she drove home.

Chapter Nine

"This concludes the sixth session of Adventures in Living Free." Mark took a deep breath and looked over the group of young people. "Deciding to live one day at a time is the most important decision you can make. It's been a great session!"

Again Mark cleared his throat of emotion. It had been an important session, as these young people finally unburdened their souls. The experience welded them into a unit of concern for each other.

Then he gave the assignment for the next meeting on developing enthusiasm. "The award winners need to take their places at the door so we can congratulate them." He caught José's eye. "I'll take you home." Somehow he hoped to break through the wall José still hid behind. Perhaps this evening had helped.

As they all stood he remembered the group wouldn't meet the next week. "Don't forget the rodeo next week!"

Mark usually felt drained after the class, but tonight he really dragged.

Lynn was putting addresses on the cards of encouragement. "You look tired tonight," she confirmed.

Noele handed him the cola he hadn't finished during

the break, and quickly they completed their chores.

"That's it for tonight. Shall I get the light?" She waited for Mark to move from the chair where he had slumped. José lingered in the hallway, propped against the wall.

"You two go ahead." Mark managed a smile. "I'll lock up."

When honest with himself Mark knew why he lacked enthusiasm, why each day seemed an eternity—Lisa Beall. How many times had he told himself he wasn't going to think of her, wasn't going to seek her out?

With Kim gone to her future in-laws he hadn't even seen Lisa, not in person, but she haunted his mind waking and sleeping. Mark stood, looking around the room, making certain he had gathered everything up. He wanted Lisa; he desired her. Yet when they were together they seemed to lunge straight for each other's throats.

Sexual attraction wasn't a firm foundation on which to build a lasting relationship. Ideals and goals in common were necessary. Foolishly he had thought he could change Lisa to suit him. From his work with teens he should have known people don't change for others. The change had to come from within. And why would Lisa Beall want to change her goals for him?

Mark approached José with a grim nod. The nineteen-year-old let Mark struggle at the door with his box of supplies and followed him sullenly into the warm summer night. The car was parked off the main drag, on a deserted street around the corner from the streetlight. With his arms full Mark couldn't point, so he said, "Car's down there, at the corner."

José spotted it but maintained his shield of silence. However, Mark could feel the young man beside him slow his pace and noticed he scanned the streets and alley carefully. Suddenly hair stood up along Mark's neck and he, too, slowed.

Mark set down the box and looked around before finally deciding there was no cause for alarm. He put the key in the trunk. Still partially bent over he was easy prey for the two attackers.

But the two men seemed surprised when José took a boxing stance and growled, "Dogs!"

As Mark tried to dodge a hamlike fist, two questions passed through his mind. *Did these men think José would join them? Or did they just think I would be alone?*

"Take the punk!" The larger attacker pounded a fist into Mark's nose. Then, he delivered heavy blows to Mark's rib cage before Mark could get in some punches himself. He grasped the man's throat. Mark's knee surprised his opponent, forcing the other off and back.

"Who are you working for?" Mark pressed his thumbs harder on the jugular.

Coming up rapidly with his arms inside Mark's, the man broke free, stumbling backward. Mark leaped on top of him. The resounding crack of heads meeting concrete left both of them dazed. Slowly Mark rose to a crawling position, trying to see through the mat of hair and blood clouding his vision.

Finally his eyes focused on José and his adversary. Somehow José had managed to pull a knife and was preparing to deliver a killing stroke. Using the last of his strength, Mark cried desperately, "No, José, no—" He lost consciousness.

José stopped his lunge in midair. The man rolled over and jumped free. Seeing his partner lying as if dead, he disappeared in the shadows.

For a moment José watched him run, breathing deeply; then flicking his switchblade shut he moved to

Mark. Feeling the pulse José looked around carefully before he dragged Mark's long frame into the back seat of the Monte Carlo. After a quick glance at the man still prone on the street, José searched the curb until he found the keys where Mark had dropped them. Then he slid into the driver's seat and decisively drove to The Bells, a safe place.

Jewel Beall seemed a solid rock in José's chaotic experience of the world. She valued him as a human being, as did *Señor* Mark. José's black eyes quickly checked the unconscious figure in the back seat.

Because Mark London had treated him as an equal, José kept attending his classes. He kept trying, even though he wondered if he would still be alive from one day to the next—or dead, like his beautiful sister, Roberta.

It was ten o'clock but a light still shone from the front of the house when José pulled into the driveway. Quickly he ran up the steps and rang the doorbell. José heard a dog inside snuffing around the facing and whining. Then Lisa opened the door, the two collies flanking her.

Seeing blood on José's hand and swelling around one eye, Lisa exclaimed, "You're hurt!"

"Not me." José gestured toward the car, his eyes pleading with her to help without too many questions. "*Señor* Mark."

"Mark!" Lisa didn't even realize she called his name as she ran after José to the car.

Pulling the front seat forward José hoisted Mark from the back. Without hesitation Lisa joined him in trying to lift Mark's long form. They had him out of the car and leaning on the side when Mark came to.

"Hey—ohhhh!" He clutched his head. Groggily he blinked down at Lisa. "Lisa?" He gave her a lopsided smile and tried to stand alone. "Lisa," he repeated her name and nodded.

He wiped across his eyes to clear his vision. The sudden movement made him sway dizzily.

José took one side and Lisa the other to walk him to the house.

"Wait. I can make it." Mark pushed them aside. This almost brought them all down as he lunged forward.

"No, *Señor*." José soothed Mark as he guided him up the stone path. "Just a minute now and *Señora* Beall, she'll take care of you."

"Why'd you bring me here?" demanded Mark, still disoriented.

"Not safe at your place."

Lisa looked at José alertly and he clamped his mouth shut. They propped Mark against the doorjamb of the screened porch while Lisa opened the door into the living room. Then as Mark's legs began to buckle under him, they half-dragged, half-carried him to the couch. They stretched him out on the divan and urged him to keep his eyes open.

"José…" Mark tried to sit up, but stopped. His head hurt too much. "You knew them. Were they after you or me?"

"Me?" José spread his hands as if not comprehending. "*Señor* Mark, they must have been after you."

Studying José's expressionless face Mark considered this for a long minute. What José said was probably true. They were attacked near his car, but somehow José figured into it.

"Mark!" Jewel hobbled in, tying her housecoat and fumbling with her glasses. "Lisa? José?" Smoothing down her hair she demanded, "What's going on?"

Lisa, kneeling beside Mark on the couch, raised her

eyes to answer, but Jewel stopped her. "I'll get alcohol and bandages."

When she had gone, Mark tried to raise himself once more. "Why did you bring me here? Did you say the Homestead isn't safe?" His eyes were blurry. He lay back, but forced out one last question to ease his mind. "You didn't kill him, José?"

"I should have." José answered grimly before sliding miserably into an easy chair. "But I didn't. Why did you stop me?" As if Mark were to blame for his troubles, he cried out, "Why didn't you let me kill him?"

The question hung in the air. Mark felt blackness overcoming him, but fought it long enough to mumble, slurring out the words, "—'cause…haunt you rest of your life…"

Thoughtfully Lisa considered the faint words; then Jewel handed her the antiseptic. Pursing her lips she stood over Mark while Lisa dabbed at the cut over his eye. "I'm calling Dr. Nelson. I don't think Mark should be moved. I believe he may have a broken rib." As she went to the phone she grumbled, "Wonder it didn't puncture his lung."

When she returned to say the doctor was coming, José stood. "I must go."

"Where do you live?" Jewel eyed the young man. She knew about Mark's juveniles. Many didn't have a home.

That habitual Latin shrug accompanied José's answer. "Someplace."

"Then stay in the greenhouse shed. There's an old bedroll out there."

His usual impassive expression slipped for a moment, revealing the leap of gratitude in his black eyes. "*Si, Señora.*" He opened his hands wide, accepting her blessing. "Thank you, thank you."

Mark came to again before the doctor arrived. This

118

time he seemed clearer except when he moved his head. Through his lashes he could see Lisa in a chair pulled close to the couch. Jewel sat across the room, crocheting.

For several minutes he watched Lisa, her hair glinting in the light of the table lamp, her eyes dark with concern. Her brow was furrowed in concentration as she stared at the book before her. He knew she wasn't reading because her eyes didn't scan the page. Becoming aware of his scrutiny, she glanced at him.

"Where's José?"

Jewel answered, her hook poised in mid-air. "He's spending the night in the greenhouse."

"Good." Holding his head steady Mark again tried to sit up.

"Lie down, Mark," Jewel ordered in her no-nonsense tone. "You may have some cracked ribs. Dr. Nelson's coming."

Taking mental inventory of his aches Mark felt inclined to agree with Jewel's diagnosis. It was agony to breathe deeply, so he obeyed and tried to wait patiently. As if drawn by a magnet his eyes went to Lisa. Steadily she met his gaze, but neither spoke.

Finally she dropped her eyes self-consciously and picked up the book, pretending to read. Mark knew she had no idea of the words before her, but he didn't care, because now he could study her. He could soak in every feature of her lovely face. He studied the slightly arching brows, the thick long lashes sweeping down to hide the embarrassment his unwavering look evoked in her brown eyes, the tiny freckles on her straight nose, the audacious dimple, the delicately curved lips—the bottom slightly larger—her defiant chin—firm above a long smooth throat—

Grudgingly he ended his inventory as Dr. Nelson arrived. Confirming Jewel's diagnosis, the doctor taped Mark up tightly. He also found a slight concussion and decreed that Mark should stay put on the couch until the next day. "Come in tomorrow for an X-ray."

After the doctor left, Jewel demanded an explanation from Mark. "We were attacked by two big men. That's all I know."

"What about José?"

"For tonight he should be safe in your greenhouse. Maybe tomorrow I can get some sense from him. He knows more than he admits." Mark was too tired to think much.

Jewel gathered up her crochet things. "Most people do." She nodded at Lisa, silently hovering near Mark. "I'll call Mrs. London so she won't worry. You get a light cover and a pillow." She turned out all the lights except the table lamp and went to her room.

Lisa spread the light flannel sheet over Mark and held the pillow tightly. She shied away from the contact. Finally firming her lips and avoiding looking at Mark she bent forward saying briskly, "Shift just a little and I'll have this placed in a moment."

That done, she stepped back and asked, "Are you comfortable?"

"Fine." Mark closed his eyes.

Lisa crossed the room to the hallway. As she turned away, Mark's lids flew open and he vacillated between calling her name and letting her go. His vow never to apologize again danced before him. But somewhere between the class this evening and his becoming an invalid on the couch Mark had decided that stiff pride and giving up never led to success. And Lisa Beall he wasn't giving up, not without a good try. "Lisa—"

The word was barely above a whisper, but a breath of air would have caught Lisa's finely attuned attention.

Quickly she turned, then paused.

He spoke her name again. "Lisa, stay. I can't sleep." Instantly she was at his side.

"Don't move! Your ribs, you might—"

Restlessly he tossed the cover. "Don't leave me." Pathetically he begged, taking full advantage of his injuries.

Lisa hastily returned to the chair she'd occupied earlier. She perched on the edge, giving him her full attention.

Perhaps because of being attacked, or because José had been so close to making a terrible mistake, Mark felt an overwhelming urge to explain about Roberta Valdez. "Lisa, I want to tell you about…" A moan escaped his lips; his head throbbed so.

"No, no!" Remembering the feeling of desolation that had crushed her at Carl's revelations she stood up and cried, "Don't talk, you shouldn't!"

"But I must." He moved, and a wave of blackness filled his head.

"No!" Lisa stood behind the chair as if it were a barrier, and her cold hand clutched her throat. "I don't want to hear." Childishly she covered her ears and started to leave the room.

"Lisa, please—"

She stopped but didn't turn.

Immediately Mark abandoned an explanation. He wasn't up to it and Lisa was distraught. "Read to me." His eyes rested on the Bible on the end table. "Stay and read."

Slowly Lisa picked up her grandmother's large print version. Calmer now she managed to ask, "What? Where?"

Beneath half-closed lids, Mark considered Lisa. "I'm trying to think. Romans. Read Romans."

"Romans?" All she could think of was seeing Mark crumpled in the back seat of the car as if dead. Her whole world had become meaningless. But he wasn't dead. He was alive and ordering her around, domineering as usual.

"Romans, the eighth chapter."

Turning to the proper place in the New Testament, Lisa said sternly. "You hush now. If you want me to stay, you'll have to be quiet."

Having achieved his purpose Mark obeyed, innocently closing his eyes. As Lisa glanced over the headings she wondered why he'd chosen this scripture. Mark always had a reason for the things he did. She began to read aloud.

For those who live according to the flesh set their minds on things of the flesh, but those who live according to the Spirit, the things of the Spirit....to be spiritually minded is life and peace.

It was very plain—and frightening.

When she reached the twenty-eighth verse, Mark asked her to read it again. "And we know that all things work together for good to those who love God, to those who are called according to His purpose."

He nodded but didn't comment so she read steadily on to the end of the chapter. "...nor any created thing, shall be able to separate us from the love of God which is in Christ Jesus our Lord."

When she finished she glanced at Mark. His lids were closed, brown lashes long, curling, and perfectly still. Was he asleep? She doubted it, but it didn't matter; she was going to her room. Lisa slowly closed the Bible and replaced it on the table.

After Mark left early the next morning, Jewel sent Lisa out with instructions to arrange the greenhouse as temporary quarters for José.

Stepping from the shed into the sunlight Lisa stretched the kinks out of her back and called back to José. "Now you should be fixed up."

José spread the raffia rug over the dirt floor, then joined her. "It's good." He looked up and whistled in amazement.

Lisa realized the sun was hazy. In the west the horizon was a brown mass, turning to black. She saw Dulce carrying a tray toward them. Then the wind hit. Stifling dust surrounded them. They all dashed for the greenhouse and José forced the door shut. Even with the door secure, dust sifted into the room around the glass panes.

"A dust storm." Dulce coughed and set the tray on a table. Black and red dirt blotted out the sun. The swirling sand outside made them feel suffocated.

Dulce pointed to the food. "I was bringing you a snack."

"We might as well share it." Lisa divided the rolls and tea. "Dig in."

José and Dulce ate self-consciously. As the silence lengthened Lisa felt she should say something, but what could the three of them have in common?

Dulce found the common denominator. To José she said, "You're in Mr. Mark's class now?"

He nodded shortly.

"How many sessions have you had?" Dulce pressed him.

"We had our sixth class last night." José's eyes brightened when he remembered the honest sharing he'd experienced.

"Oh, that's the one where you talk about things that

have been worrying you." Dulce would never forget what she had learned.

José twirled a roll on its side. "And we talked about living one day at a time." From his manner they could see he was working through something in his mind. "That is the way it must be. One day at a time."

"Exactly." Dulce's almond-shaped eyes admired José. "You do like the classes then?"

Ruefully José smiled, a flash of white teeth in his brown face. "At first they are frightening and you hate going, but soon the fear goes away."

"Mr. Mark is wonderful! I did not know of his hurt until this morning and he had already gone home." Her lovely eyes begged for reassurance about the condition of her hero.

Of course, Lisa assured herself, Dulce had every reason to idolize Mark. He found her a job and helped her straighten out her life. Even knowing this, Lisa couldn't keep from saying cynically, "The know-it-all man is indestructible."

"Know-it-all man?" Puzzled at this phrase, Dulce cocked her head at Lisa and repeated the words. "Know-it-all man." They became a blessing rather than an epithet. Thoughtfully she nodded in agreement. "Yes, he does, I believe."

Disgusted with such blatant worship of the one man who had ever caused her any soul-searching, Lisa emphasized, "He thinks he does, anyway."

Neither Dulce nor José seemed to realize Lisa was being sarcastic. José broke the thoughtful silence. "He doesn't know everything, I see, but he does know about the most important things, about living and dying."

Lisa gave up. What could she say in opposition to such admiration? Nothing. Her mind swirled like the sand outside the greenhouse glass.

The morning of the rodeo Mark ordered José to remain at The Bells. Lisa was working on her autoharp when José came to the greenhouse in search of a yard tool. She tried to comfort him. "Don't feel bad, José; I'm sure Mark had a good reason for asking you to stay here."

"Oh yes, he had a good reason!" José tilted his head back and clasped his forehead dramatically.

Lisa stared at his surprising animation.

He continued miserably, hanging his head in shame, "It is all my fault!"

"What have you done?"

Wildly he flung his hands out. "Mr. Mark is being followed because of me. I am hiding and he's in danger!"

At Lisa's wide-eyed concern José came to his senses. Grabbing a hoe he ran from the greenhouse. She started to follow, to question him, but knew it would be futile.

Mark was in danger. This much she knew. Chills swept up and down her spine as she thought of this, a palpable terror. Beside her autoharp lay a New Testament.

When Lisa picked it up the pages parted at Romans. She could feel Mark's presence there on the pages. She reread the scripture she'd read for Mark the night he was attacked. The closing verses helped quiet her fears: "Who shall separate us from the love of Christ? Will tribulation, distress, or persecution?" She knew that nothing could separate Mark from loving his God.

Closing the book and propping her chin in her hands Lisa stared into space. She recalled meeting Mark on the road, Mark playing tennis, Mark rescuing her from the bullets, Mark kissing her the night after she sang. Then

125

she'd been too pig-headed to admit her ecstasy, even to herself.

Thinking of Mark and of that night made Lisa's mind turn to the new song she was writing. It had lain dormant for weeks because she couldn't concentrate on the lyrics.

But now the melody hummed in her brain. Phrases began to gather like rainclouds before a storm. "The Spirit bears witness…we are children of God." Lisa could feel the words coming.

Oh, Son of God, I look up to you,
You hang so cruelly on that tree,
How could you have gone so far to prove
You love a child like me?

Singing the first verse again Lisa tested its texture. She wanted this next verse to develop the original thought. The first verse used the example of the sun; the second, the moon. Now for the contrast. "With your life you daily show me the way." What next?

Warm. Somehow she'd like to tie that in with the first stanza. "Warm, your tender love that burns within." Hurriedly she scribbled the words on the pad lest she forget.

She had the third verse almost complete. But what would constitute the fourth? The second verse, about the moon, needed a contrast, too, or an expansion. Suddenly Lisa felt mentally exhausted, drained. Nothing more would appear.

She slumped back in her chair and glanced at the clock. It was time to get dressed for the rodeo.

When Kim called to tell Lisa she was taking Mark and would pick her up early, Lisa didn't even question his going. If Mark was in danger, she could try to protect him.

At the gate to the rodeo grounds, they were waved through by the attendant who at first failed to recognize Mark.

Kim laughed at her brother when he disgustedly returned his pass to his billfold. "You've got to be kidding. After all the work you've done getting this rodeo together, how could anyone not know you?"

Kim parked the Monte Carlo inside the arena compound. Before the dust even settled around the car, two people appeared with problems. A harried Girl Scout leader had trouble in the snack stand. "The ice machine is broken down."

Mark nodded and started to follow her and her troop. But a man with pliers and a roll of electrical wiring stopped him. "One of the speakers isn't working. We may need some parts."

"Get what you need and keep the sales ticket. Is that all?"

"Someone up in the announcer's booth was asking about stop watches." He called back over his shoulder, already heading toward the broken speaker.

Kim waved a sack and some papers she had pulled from the car. "I'll take the watches and the record sheets and try to get things together there."

Lisa stood halfway between the car where Kim was and Mark who was walking to the snack stand.

Mark spoke to the troop leader. "I'll be there in a sec." He spotted a van pulling through the gates. "There's the candy man now, and no, we don't charge tax." Then he came back toward Lisa. "I need you with me to write down what has to be done and help me coordinate things."

Realizing an opportunity to discover who threatened Mark, Lisa volunteered. "I can be the gopher."

"Good." Kim waved and took off across the arena.

Lisa ignored his incredulous expression and smiled angelically. She trailed him to the refreshment stand. One side opened out and up to offer protection from the wind and rain. While Mark went through the invoices Lisa introduced herself to the Scout leader. "What do we need to do first?"

"If you can help these three girls get the popcorn machine going, we'll open candy boxes and get them displayed." She smiled her gratitude.

Lisa measured popcorn into the large machine along with the special mix of butter and salt. As it spewed forth the fluffy white corn they scooped it into red-striped sacks and placed them on the warming pan ready for impatient customers.

"I'll start another batch and you tell me the correct measures." The bright-eyed girl dressed in jeans, official shirt, and badge sash nodded intelligently.

Soon the Scouts were doing fine, so Lisa decided to check out the ice machine, since Mark was still busy with a steady flow of questions. As she traced the electric cord and found it plugged in, it occurred to her to check the breaker box. Soon the machine was purring and the ice chips began to pile up. She put some in a cup and munched on them as she joined Mark at the entrance.

"Mr. Mark!" Two older girls in Western outfits hovered near. "Where do you want us to work?"

Before he gave their assignments he noticed Lisa. "What have you there?"

She held the cup so he could see. "Ice. Want some?"

"Looks good." He shook out a bite, tilting the cup back and letting the chips fall into his mouth. Returning the cup he looked at it curiously. "The ice machine is running?"

"I fixed it." She laughed and swung her denim shoulder bag over one arm, then flirtatiously wrapped her other arm through his.

The two girls observed this with envy and admiration. Suddenly aware of their awed expressions Mark assigned them their jobs. He looked at Lisa speculatively but didn't say anything; instead he pulled her closer to his side as they swung over a raised step.

She reminded herself that she was doing all this to protect Mark, but she had difficulty thinking at all with him smiling down at her in that caressing way.

"How are we judging the sheep penning?" A man with a badge on his shirt was studying a sheet of paper. Mark explained the requirements and sent the man on his way.

To Lisa he said, "Remind me to go over these points with George Mahon so he can announce them with each event."

As they progressed slowly toward the announcer's booth, Mark asked Lisa to remind him of this or that or someone who needed to be seen about something. On the third reminder she dug in her purse for a pad and noted his instructions.

When they were alone for a moment he pointed at the pad and pen stuck in her shirt pocket and smiled, "Miss Efficiency."

"Your right-hand man, remember." Their eyes met in laughter and held. Her knees began to melt into jelly. She swallowed and brightly suggested, "Forward ho!" taking his arm once more. When she was beside him, it was easier to avoid Mark's eyes.

There were two ways up to the speaker's perch, a rung ladder at one end and a spiral metal staircase at the other. With Mark's injury in mind, they chose the stairs. They met Sheila Richardson-Baird and Mark's mother at the top. "Mo—Edwina and Sheila. Right on time." Mark assisted Edwina up the last step of the staircase. "Lisa, could you set up some folding chairs?"

Counting slowly to ten, Lisa nodded at Sheila and smiled politely at Edwina. Then she took two of the metal chairs and set them up behind the long table. Suddenly music blasted all around them. Mark scrambled for the controls where a young man was sitting. He turned it down and grinned. "The speaker's working now!"

A cowhand clanged up the staircase shouting for Mark. "Where are the flags to lead off the grand entry?"

"In the trunk of my car." Mark pulled the keys from his Levi's pocket. "I'll go with you and make one last check around."

Immediately Lisa picked up her purse. "I'll go, too." She flushed at Sheila's sardonic glance but didn't back down.

The late July sun had not set when the rodeo began. Perhaps because of the beautiful weather and the knowledge that their money would go for a good cause, there was a holiday spirit in the air. One event succeeded another. First were the calf-roping, steer riding, and barrel races. At the end came the bull-riding because of its very real danger and audience appeal. Throughout, the excitement remained high.

Mark, Lisa, Kim when not dashing off, Edwina, Sheila and a dozen other people occupied the review stand. Each event passed smoothly. Finally it was time for the bull-riding. Lisa could feel the tension in the booth as the men in the chutes readied the first rider.

Mark stood through most of the rodeo, moving continually to check on things, clambering up and down on errands, or in a moment of respite leaning at the corner of the front window out of everyone's way. While George Mahon gave the statistics of each rider and bull, Sheila joined Mark at the opening.

"I'm so glad you decided to let your foreman be the clown tonight." She placed a possessive hand on Mark's arm. "My heart just stops beating whenever you're the clown."

Patting her hand and smiling at Sheila with that slow crooked grin that so upset Lisa's pulse-rate, Mark assured her, "If you're careful there's not much danger. Lee's a good man and won't take any unnecessary risks."

Sheila delicately shuddered, "But the necessary ones are just as frightening."

Lisa, now aware that Mark must often be a rodeo clown, took particular interest in the event below. Mark's foreman took desperate chances with his life, tantalizing the bull by dancing in front of him in his baggy jeans and red flannel shirt. He waved a red flag defiantly before the snorting nose, diving out of the way of a charge at the last second or sometimes jumping into a wooden barrel.

Lisa had of course seen rodeos at home in Oklahoma, but she had never studied the dangerous role of the rodeo clown.

Now Lisa realized the clown had to make instant decisions concerning his life and the life of the contestant. He had to be agile, surefooted, and a man of steel will and courage. He also had to value his life less than the lives of the others. Edwina looked at her strangely when Lisa collapsed in a chair with a sigh at the end of the final ride.

While the band played and the field was cleared,

Sheila made her way to the arena. She was to present the ribbons and prizes and was dressed for the occasion in a russet skirt and vest of Western styling. A large turquoise necklace encircled her throat. Of course, Sheila required Mark's assistance to pick her way across the dirt and manure to the platform which had been dragged by a tractor to the center of the arena. With Mark beside her she bestowed the awards, coyly kissing the young men and sending them into blushes.

Sheila remained on the platform as the driver slowly pulled it from the field, waving like a queen on a parade float. Her exit was the signal for the crowd to rise. With a satisfied air people surged from the stands.

Lisa carried Edwina's purse and jacket as they negotiated the narrow spiral case. At the bottom Edwina took her things. "Everything went very well," she said as if claiming part of the credit. "Mark should be pleased." She looked at Lisa brightly, "For his juveniles, you know."

Lisa nodded, her eyes searching for Kim who had been almost as difficult to keep track of as Mark. Mark! She had lost him in the crowd. Standing on tiptoe she looked around. Kim saw her and waved, making her way across to them.

"Ah, Kimberly, here you are." Edwina fondly patted her daughter's hand. "You and Mark did a marvelous job."

"Thank you." Kim smiled impishly. "It went pretty well."

"When will you be home?"

"Ages!" Kim rolled her eyes. "Still tons to do."

Sheila joined them then. "Where's Mark?"

"He was packing up the leftover ribbons the last time I saw him." Kim checked an item off her list and turned to go.

"Would you tell him I'm ready to leave?" Sheila looked down at her high heels.

"I'm tired, too." Edwina coughed as the wind picked up some dirt and swirled it around them.

Kim stopped and shook her head. "My advice is for you two to go on. My list is a mile long and I'm sure Mark has even more things to do."

For a moment Sheila hesitated, then said, "You'll tell Mark I took your mother home, won't you?" She smiled sweetly and took Edwina's arm. "Workaholics. Let's go have some iced tea."

The receipts had to be counted, the refreshment stand cleaned and closed, the unused articles returned or stored, and the speaker system dismantled.

Lisa and Kim helped with everything. Lisa was glad she had worn jeans and a shirt even though she'd felt over-shadowed by Sheila's russet skirt and vest. When they had done everything they could, they simply had to wait. Mark's personal gratitude and thanks to the people who had donated time and effort had to come from him.

"My feet hurt." Kim bowed her legs and stood on the sides of her boots, her face comically grimacing. "I'm going to the car."

Since nothing the least bit suspicious had happened, Lisa was feeling her fears for Mark were foolish. She found a spot up in the bleachers where she could keep an eye on him. He was mingling with the contestants still loading their horses in vans. She took a deep breath and looked around the arena.

As Lisa stood in the empty bleachers, the stadium bare of human form and color, she was reminded of a theater after a performance, suddenly devoid of any life. Desolation swept over her, a bleak question: "Is that all there is?" She wanted to cry. Lisa willed the tears

133

away and cleared her throat of a lump, but the sadness, the sense of futility stayed with her.

Slowly she descended the steps, watching the last dust from the departing vans settle to the ground. Studying her feet as she stepped down Lisa was unaware that Mark stood at the bottom until he extended a hand to help her down the last step. Startled she glanced up, and he saw the residue of tears on her lids.

"Lisa." The way he said her name always made her stomach muscles tighten. "Why the tears?"

Of all things at this moment she didn't want tenderness from Mark London—the man who had upset her whole world, making her achingly aware of its frail glories.

"Leave me alone." She shook off his helping hand and turned away.

He followed her silently, but when she stumbled he reached out to catch her. "Lisa, what's wrong?"

"Can't you see I just want to be alone?" She faced him, daring him to offer sympathy. The tears ran down her face unchecked. Folding her arms across her chest she glared at him.

He reached out and caught a tear on his finger. "Can't I help, Lisa?"

She stepped quickly back, shuddering slightly. "You've already done enough to mess up my life, Mark London. Just leave me alone."

His jaw flexed; his lids shuttered his eyes. Then tilting his hat down he pivoted, striding to the car, leaving her to follow alone.

Chapter Ten

Jewel's light was still on beneath the door when Lisa arrived home from the rodeo, so she tapped lightly.

"Come in." Jewel sat up straighter in bed and put down the book she had been reading. "How was the rodeo? Did they have a good crowd?"

"There was a mob!" After giving her grandmother a quick hello peck on the cheek, Lisa perched on the bed. She longed to go straight to her room, but her grandmother looked forward so much to a report of her doings that Lisa put aside her own feelings and tried to make the event come alive for her.

"Everything went well. At first one of the speakers was broken and the ice machine didn't work. But Mark got it all together, and he was very pleased with the gate." Lisa propped her hands behind her head and lay back on the bed. "The evening was beautiful and we didn't need jackets. The stock was fresh."

"Mark wasn't the clown, was he?"

When Jewel anxiously asked this question Lisa knew she had been right. Mark was often the clown. "With his ribs? Besides, he had too much else to do since it was his show."

"He works too hard."

135

Lisa sat up. "Sheila Richardson-Baird presented the awards."

Jewel didn't comment but she raised her eyebrows.

"She arrived with Mrs. London." Lisa paused again. "Has she…how long…she's very attractive." Finally she met Jewel's eyes.

"They practically grew up together." No need to explain the *they*. "At one time everyone thought they would make a match of it. That was before…" Jewel stopped and looked at Lisa.

Lisa quickly stood up and said, "I've kept you up monstrously late. We'll talk more tomorrow." Hastily she left Jewel and stumbled down the hall to her room. The truth was Lisa wanted to hear what Jewel would say, but knew a surge of sympathy and compassion for Mark would be the result. And she couldn't take anything more this evening.

On her dresser sat her mail. In the rush getting ready for the rodeo she hadn't read it. The handwriting on one of the letters caught her eye. Reluctantly she picked up the envelope and looked at the return address.

It was from Brad Golwan, the leader of The Wind. She stared at the postmark. Could it be the middle of July already? Where had the days gone? Suddenly Lisa was crying. What had she done with the days? What was she going to do? Did she still not know where she was going? With the envelope hanging limply in her hand, Lisa curled up in the faded old rose pattern of the chintz chair.

Through tears she visualized their last concert together, a fantastic, exhilarating experience. They had received a standing ovation and been persuaded to perform encore after encore. The students—their classmates—had begged for more. Lisa had thought that marvelous, glowing feeling would never dim, nor be exceeded. But it had.

Vividly Lisa remembered singing on George Mahon's show. The viewing audience had been large, but for her there had been a small audience of one—Mark London. She hadn't realized it then, only now, when a decision was required of her. The decision could wait, for several weeks, in fact. But that wouldn't be fair to the group. They should know what to plan on. Was she going to tour with them or not? If she didn't, what would she do? Could she live without singing? Honesty compelled the answer. She *had* to sing. But this summer she had found several places to sing—with the church group, on local television, and soon for Kim's wedding. And there was a certain joy in singing alone in her greenhouse retreat.

On the other side of the coin was this question, would she be happy touring with the group? All over the country, in one motel after another, night after dreary night? They would be playing the small towns and hoping for the big ones to come, struggling for national recognition, for a hit record, and all the while the jealousies of the group would be wearing her nerves to the end. Before coming to New Mexico, Lisa had thought she could bear all the tedium because of the ultimate fame. Before this summer, her grandmother, Kim, and...Mark.

Her thinking had changed. Jewel, Kim, and Mark had influenced her, but they weren't totally responsible. Lisa had changed within. Now the appeal of fame and fortune flickered so far away and so faintly she knew it would soon be extinguished. Another light had entered her life. At first, she had been blinded by it. She had rebelled, but gradually Lisa had adjusted to what she saw, knowing this light would never go out. Jesus, the Son of

137

God, was the light and in Him was no darkness.

After ripping open the envelope, Lisa unfolded the paper.

> I hope your summer hasn't seemed as long as mine. To fill in the time I've written some new stuff and can hardly wait for us to get together to try it out. I know we all agreed to rest this summer and think about the future for real. I've thought, and it's the group for me. I've even got us a show for August 26. We'll need to order new outfits and rehearse like mad.
>
> Lisa, are you with us? You know we want you, but when school was out you held back. How do you feel now? If you think you're in, then gung ho!
>
> Eager to hear from you,
>
> Brad
>
> PS. Wait till you hear my new songs!

Letting the pages drift to the night table, Lisa thought of the song she had been writing. Never had one eluded her so, nor grown so agonizingly. She had struggled with it all summer. One more verse would complete it. How would it end?

She couldn't write Brad tonight. She was exhausted. Tomorrow she would tackle the letter. Probably she'd mull the letter over until she went crazy weighing one side against the other, but she didn't. As if drugged, she fell instantly asleep.

Awaking early the next morning, Lisa firmly wrote the reply. It was brief and to the point and carried little of the agony of her decision.

The days have zipped by. It seems impossible that July is almost over. You are right about needing to know what I plan to do now. In a letter I can't explain all the reasons for my decision. It's not an easy one, but I cannot join you. I'm replying immediately so you will have enough time to find a replacement.

Thank you and tell the others, although I will write them, that I remember great times together and wish you all the best.

Love,

Lisa

Determined to mail the note immediately before she could change her mind, Lisa quickly dressed. She called to Jewel that she was running in to town and would be back soon.

"I need some milk." Jewel came to the living room and called up the stairs, "I didn't realize I was out and started a chocolate pie. Would you mind?"

"Of course not! Anything else?" Lisa stuffed the envelope in her bag, slinging it casually over her shoulder as if it contained nothing of importance, certainly nothing that would change the course of her destiny. It hit her then that it was the little things in life that made all the difference. The insight frightened her.

Anxiously, she looked down the staircase at Jewel wiping her hands on the towel, at the sunlight shining in the window, at the green spot of potted plants in the corner. It was all the same, but she would remember this moment for the rest of her life.

Jewel looked up at Lisa and smiled. "I can't think of anything else I need right now. Probably the minute you're gone, I will." Giving Lisa a kiss on her cheek as she passed, Jewel sent her off with a wave.

Opening the car windows Lisa let her hair blow, blocking out any thinking with the noise. When she reached town she noticed it was so hot the black asphalt already oozed in the heat. A cola would be good...no, no putting off the deed. Mail it and be done with it.

Pulling into the drive-through postal area Lisa held the envelope in her hand, flipping it thoughtfully. She scrutinized the address, the stamp, the correct return. All in order. Now for the irrevocable step.

Pulling out the metal handle on the post box Lisa laid the letter on the flat surface. She let it go like a hot potato. As the lid banged shut with a hollow reverberation inside, she heard the swish of the paper sliding down, down, down.

Through tears Lisa guided the car to McDonald's. Smudging her eyes dry she entered the restaurant feeling she had no friend in the world.

"Just the person I've been searching for," said a smooth voice.

Raising her saddened eyes Lisa encountered Carl Valdez. He placed a cold drink on her table and confiscated the stool across from her. Somehow Carl Valdez wasn't entirely satisfactory in the role of friend. Beggars can't be choosers, she reminded herself and smiled.

"I looked everywhere for you at the rodeo." His brown eyes tried to hold hers, but she was in no mood for flirtatious games.

"Most of the time I was in the announcer's booth." *Following Mark around like a fool*, Lisa added to herself. *Much he needed me to protect him!* "It's hot, isn't it?" She thought the weather might do to fill the silence.

"*Mucho!*" Carl wiped imaginary sweat from his brow. "The crowd was huge." He returned to the subject of

140

the rodeo. "Mark London seems to have sponsored another winner." Moodily he forgot his pose of male interest and stirred his tea.

All Lisa could think of was their last meeting when Carl insisted on telling her about Mark killing his wife. Just remembering made her nauseous. Quickly she sipped her carbonated drink, trying to come up with an exit line.

"Has that José kid been around?" Carl picked up his tea and drank but watched her beneath his lids.

"José?"

"You know." Carl set down the cup. "He showed up at the engagement party looking for Mark."

A sudden prickle along her skin gave Lisa a feeling of unease. She wondered, *Why is Carl so concerned with José?*

Drawing another swallow through the straw, Lisa could clearly see José before her, almost demented with fear for Mark—and himself—the night Mark had been attacked.

"I can't seem to place him. Most of the people at the party I had never seen before."

"Lisa!" Kim strode eagerly across the tile floor. She nodded politely at Carl. Putting down her purse and taking out some coins, she ordered, "Don't move a muscle, I'll get my drink and join you."

Returning with her drink Kim enthused, "The rodeo was a great success! Ann took tons of pictures for a full page spread today. That reminds me, I never did get you that clipping. We have copies galore at the house now." She looked at the other two, now that her news was out. "What's new?"

Lisa gestured negatively and sipped her cola. She couldn't tell Kim about the letter in front of Carl.

Carl, using a deliberately casual tone, asked, "Did you

hear about the beer truck that was hijacked?"

Glad of any subject Kim leaned forward to show interest.

Lisa raised an eyebrow. "But that was over a month ago."

"It was?" Kim was determined to follow some topic of conversation.

"The day of the funeral. Remember?" Lisa recalled the day vividly. "Mark and I heard it on the car radio just as we arrived. Why did you ask? Have they discovered something more?"

"No." Carl waved a hand negligently. "Nothing."

Still in the dark and feeling miffed, Kim was about to demand, "Then why on earth did you bring it up?" when Carl changed the subject himself.

"Where is Mark? He should be celebrating his successful rodeo."

Kim could always talk about Mark. "I tried to get him to break free and come to town with me. But he had some work to do before he took off at noon today for Albuquerque."

Why did this knowledge make Lisa's stomach sink to the floor? "Mark's going to Albuquerque?" She had planned to tell him of her decision; now he was leaving without a word to her. But after last night, could she have expected otherwise?

Why had she been in such haste to mail her letter to Brad? She should have waited. Now her bridges were burned. The letter was gone, and so was Mark London.

Lisa opened the screen door and stood still for a moment relishing the coolness of the house after the hot car.

But Jewel had heard the door, for she called, "Lisa. Good. Now I'll finish the pies."

Disgusted with herself Lisa responded, "I forgot the milk. I'm sorry. I could go back in—"

"Don't. It's too hot to stand over a stove anyway."

"Where are you?"

"On the back porch. Shelling blackeyes. Come on out."

Now Lisa understood the pinging noise she'd heard. Putting her purse on the stairs she went through the kitchen to the back.

"There's another pan." Jewel's fingers never missed a beat as she snapped the ends off and quickly stripped the hulls.

Lisa's pile seemed to remain the same while Jewel's grew rapidly. But Lisa didn't have her mind on her work. Instead, today she listened to Jewel reminiscing. She was telling some anecdote about Kim learning to make cookies.

"She forgot to put in the baking soda." Her fingers still moving, Jewel glanced at Lisa and they shared a smile. "Kim cried and cried because they were hard and lumpy. Mark bravely ate them anyway, assuring her they weren't that bad." Momentarily the fingers stopped their work as Jewel rested her hands on the edge of the pan. "Darling Mark, never wanting anything hurt." She held the pea in her hand and didn't move.

Lisa raised her head to discover Jewel watching her. This was the moment. Lisa knew this was the underlying reason she had joined her grandmother to shell peas. She wanted to know what the innuendos, the unfinished phrases referred to.

Before Lisa could speak, Jewel asked, "Has anyone told you what happened to Mark?"

"Happened to Mark? I was under the impression it was something Mark *did*, not something that happened to him."

"Who told you that?" Carefully Jewel began another pod.

"Carl Valdez."

"Ah, yes, Carl." Jewel shelled several more peas. They ricocheted off the sides of the metal pan.

Trying to be patient, Lisa picked up another handful.

"Our families homesteaded this land. My Jim was like an older brother to Jeff London. When he married a woman from Dallas I tried to befriend her, but Edwina hated ranch life. When Mark was nine she became pregnant again. After nearly dying the first time, she didn't want the baby and was terrified. Then the home in Dallas burned, and her parents were killed in the fire. It took her a long time to get over it all."

Lisa's fingers were becoming more adept. She was surprised at how much her pile had grown as she became more absorbed in Jewel's recollections. She was glad to have this background on Mark.

"In his solitary explorations Mark often came here. We shared lots of milk and cookies over triumphs and tears. When Kim was able to toddle, Mark brought her along too."

Kim had said they came every day after school. No wonder Jewel had influenced their lives.

"When Mark was seventeen, he went through a period of rebelling against everything. His steady girl was Sheila—"

Her low voice stopped as Jewel let that sink in. Lisa nodded.

"One night they'd been drinking at a drive-in theater. As they came to an open stretch of road Mark decided to test his car. He reached top speed as a figure appeared on the road. His reactions were slowed. He slammed on the brake, tried to swerve, but he hit Roberta Valdez."

"Carl's wife." Lisa spoke the words to make them

real. "What was she doing in the road?"

"Carl says a party was in progress at his home. They had also been drinking. Playfully he chased her and she ran into the road. He has never let Mark forget what happened."

"Sheila was along?"

"Yes." Jewel's eyes dropped to the green pod in her hand. She didn't know what had happened, but Mark had never really had a girlfriend since. "When Sheila was twenty-three she married John Baird, a widower. Now she's a wealthy widow."

Gathering a new bunch of peas and sorting the snaps from the shells in her lap, Jewel said, "I wonder if Mark will ever marry? His dedication to young people is totally consuming. Of course, the accident seemed to be the making of him. It gave him a purpose for his life, but Mark deserves more."

Lisa didn't respond. The story had filled her heart and mind with a picture of the young boy who had become a determined, forceful man.

The next afternoon beneath the shade of a large willow, Lisa rolled over, propping her chin in her hands.

Kim, on her back, stared up through the branches. "You amaze me, Lisa. If I hadn't nagged you to death, you'd never have told me about sending that letter off to Brad." Sitting up and crossing her legs she shook her head. "I thought we were friends."

"It's hard to talk about it." Yesterday Lisa had bitterly regretted her decision, but today, she only felt some remorse. Already she was accepting the finality of her action.

"What are you going to do then?" Kim had her life so planned she couldn't imagine anyone being happy without a definite goal.

145

Lisa laughed. "Kim! For one day, I can be in limbo. Besides, I'm too tired after our tennis game to think right now." She traced the pattern on the Lone Star quilt with her finger. She had laughed spontaneously. "I'll make it. Don't worry."

"I try not to worry. You do seem in a better mood today. Yesterday you were a bear!" Kim stood and picked up her tennis bag. "I've got to run. More consultations on wedding paraphernalia." She rolled her eyes in her mischievous way and they laughed together.

Lying back on the quilt, Lisa watched the shifting shade for a long time after Kim left. Then the glare forced her to close her eyes, and small sun spots glittered inside her lids.

She thought of the sun and the contrast she had used in her song. "Oh, Son of God, I look up to you hanging there on a tree." She hummed the next phrase. "With your life you daily show me the way." Then Lisa tried to put into words her feelings about personal inner changes. "Like the moon—I prove the Son is still around."

Saying it out loud made it mean more somehow. So she continued trying to speak her thoughts. "Some glimmer of what is really important in life made me request this summer to think. I can see that now. I've only begun to study my Bible and see the larger light. But it beckons me."

Now, Lisa knew where she was going. She also knew how she would finish her song.

I hope they can from me His message learn
And though my life is short
And I'm nothing on my own
I'm still a living promise of His return.
I'm a mirror of the brightness of the Son.

I'll shine like a living promise until He comes:
May they see in me the brightness of Your Son—

Realizing the song had a distinctive John Denver flavor Lisa repeated the stanza. An inner tingling, a strange other-world feeling came over her as she sang; saying the words of her song out loud was a promise.

"Lisa!"

The voice seemed to come from far away. Blinking, Lisa opened her eyes. Her grandmother was calling her. "Coming!" Quickly she gathered up the quilt and the tea glasses.

She was placing the glasses on the table when the telephone rang. "I'll get it!"

Dragging the quilt behind her into the hall she answered, "Beall residence."

"Lisa Beall please, long distance calling."

"This is Lisa Beall."

"Miss Beall." The voice was deep and male. "Jerome Thames with Christian Broadcasting Corporation here in Albuquerque. We recently viewed a tape of your performance on George Mahon's show."

Lisa leaned against the wall and hugged the quilt close.

"We'd like to fly you here for an audition. Perhaps do a tape for our weekly show. Would you be interested?"

"Who did you…what did you say?" Lisa's voice was a croaking sound.

"Would you fly up for an audition?"

Lisa thought she caught a hint of sympathy in his tone. "Audition? To sing?" Lisa screamed in joy. "*Yes*!"

"Good." She heard him flicking pages before he spoke again. "How does July 29 sound? You'll need to fly in the day before. I'll arrange for your room and send your ticket to you."

Lisa did a little calendar calculating herself. "July 29 sounds fine. How many songs should I prepare?"

"Five or six should give us a good sampling."

"Five or six!" Nonchalantly Mr. Thames seemed to think she would have so many at her fingertips. Somehow she would.

"They needn't all be hymns. The songs should carry a message of love and hope." He paused then added, "Any questions?"

Hundreds, thousands, millions were on the tip of her tongue, but none would articulate. Finally Lisa said, "No."

"If you think of any, please feel free to call me." He gave the number and Lisa nearly dropped the phone in trying to write it down. "I'll send a letter immediately confirming our conversation and look forward to meeting you in person on July 28."

"Yes." The line went dead. And now Lisa wondered desperately what she would wear. Wear? This practical thought made Lisa question if the conversation had been real. The whole time Mr. Thames was speaking to her, it had seemed she was somewhere other than the hallway. Then her eyes focused on the receiver still clutched in her trembling hand, and she knew the call had been real, very real. A bubble of joy formed in her throat. A chance to sing on Christian Broadcasting! What an opportunity!

"Grandmother!" Cradling the receiver, she nearly tripped over the quilt. "*Grandmother*!"

"In the kitchen, dear. Who was that on the phone?"

Still trailing the quilt like a security blanket she leaned against the facing of the kitchen door and took a deep breath. "Grandmother." Awe at what had come into her life made Lisa speak with more control. "I've been invited to audition for Christian Broadcasting on July 29. Can you believe it?"

"Of course I believe it." Jewel nodded, her eyes wise. "You deserve the chance. Your lovely voice should be used for God's glory." Jewel closed the lid on another jar of green beans. "I've thought so all along."

This stopped Lisa's dancing about in mid-stride. "Grandmother, did you?"

"No, but I do wish I had thought of it. What did they say?" She loaded the jars into the pressure cooker. Sighing, Lisa slid into a chair, trying to assimilate the news. Jewel turned down the burner under the cooker and wiped her hands. She sat across from Lisa. "Now, tell me all about it."

Lisa repeated the conversation as best she could.

When she finished, Jewel muttered, "George Mahon—well!" Taking Lisa's smooth young hands into her own workworn ones, she gripped them tightly and smiled through glad tears. "My prayers have been answered." Studying the face she'd come to love more than her very breath, and unaware of Lisa's rejection letter to Brad, Jewel asked, "But you, are you glad?"

Lisa could only nod; the depth of her emotion made words impossible. Even if she failed at this audition, Lisa knew what she could work toward, for now she had a goal. Without love or singing her life wouldn't be worth living. Although her love had not yet found her, she did have her singing. She returned the pressure of the fragile hands. "Very glad. And so thankful."

Chapter Eleven

When the tennis ball whizzed past her head, Lisa blinked. She had been daydreaming about her audition instead of concentrating on the game. Chasing after the bright yellow ball she returned it to Kim. "Score?"

"My add." Kim served again, exactly on the center line.

"You aced me." Lisa smiled ruefully. "Your set, four-six."

"You weren't paying attention." Kim didn't pursue it. "I can't play tennis anymore before the wedding."

And I fly out tomorrow. At least that problem was solved easily. Lisa snapped the plastic lid on the can of balls.

"I need the exercise and it relieves the tension." Kim zipped the cover over her racket head. "Four more days and everything is changed."

"Nothing stays the same." At one time Lisa might have felt bitter about that, but now she knew it was for the best.

Kim nodded. What Lisa said was true. "I've still got tons of things to do."

"Can I help?" Lisa had things she should do too, but if Kim needed her they could wait.

"Mother is the problem." Kim sighed and picked up

her bag. "I have to keep my finger in everything to make sure she doesn't get too extravagant." But instead of moving toward the house Kim caught Lisa's arm. "Lisa, you know if I could...I hate to have you sad, worried, whatever?"

"Oh, Kim." Lisa felt guilty. "I'm not sad. I'm gloriously thrilled and scared. I've been given an exciting chance. I haven't said anything because I'm so afraid I'll fail."

"What *are* you talking about!"

"I can't." Lisa shook her head. "No, I *can* but I'd rather not. When it's over, then I'll explain."

"You're talking in riddles. At least your eyes are shining now. You've resembled gloom and doom often enough lately." Kim tilted back her visor and linked her arm with Lisa's. They walked together back to the house. "Are you singing?"

Lisa grunted an affirmative, "Uh huh."

Remembering her friend's recent rejection of singing with The Wind, Kim probed, "What sort?"

"Inspirational."

"Good." Impulsively she stopped and hugged Lisa. They laughed together over the moment of closeness and skipped the rest of the way.

On her way home Lisa was relieved she had confessed as much as she had to Kim. She jogged the last bit of the way, just because she felt the need. Out of breath she stopped beneath a large pecan tree near the back gate of The Bells. Voices attracted her attention.

Dulce was pleading with José. "You *must* tell Mr. Mark what you know! Your life, his life—all in danger." Eloquently she begged. Then she launched into persuasion in Spanish which Lisa couldn't understand.

Brushing Dulce aside, José turned toward the house. "I'm taking care of Mr. Mark."

Dulce followed, her voice fading as they moved away.

Lisa gripped the tennis bag and supported herself against the tree. Instantly she visualized Mark's crumpled body in the back seat of the Monte Carlo. Then she remembered how foolish she had felt following him around at the rodeo. When he visited Jewel now, Lisa was always gone with Kim. Obviously he was avoiding her. She could do nothing, except pack her suitcase and go sing her heart out.

In Albuquerque, standing in the barn-like studio waiting to be called, Lisa felt like a walking dream. She was actually here, moving, talking, and going through the accepted motions. But Lisa saw it all through a glass, as if she were on the outside looking in.

Entering the sound room, Lisa walked directly to the mike stand and awaited instructions. Four men, including Jerome Thames, came in and occupied some folding chairs. It always amazed Lisa how temporary these buildings looked. Except for the microphone, an old desk, the two cameras, and the folding chairs, the room was empty.

After he introduced her to the other men, Mr. Thames asked her to sing her first number. "Then wait three minutes or so for the red light to flash again and go into the next and so on until we stop you." They were planning to tape the audition.

Gripping the mike in her hand, Lisa frantically tried to recall the beginning word of her first song. Her mind was a blank. Her free hand tightened in the folds of her green dress, the dress she had worn on the George Mahon show. Closing her eyes and drawing a shuddering breath of prayer, Lisa opened them to feel Mark's presence beside her, his hand bracing her, his voice encouraging her as he had done before.

Taking another breath Lisa began, "Amazing grace, how sweet the sound..." Lisa's voice rang full and strong in her ears. She forgot the men, her fears, everything but the song she sang.

Finally she began singing her own lyrics, "Mirror of Brightness."

O Sun, I look up to you,
You hang so peacefully in the sky—

As she sang, Lisa relived the past months. She remembered her original feelings, her impetuous decision in coming to her grandmother, her certainty that she could find what she wanted from life by herself.

O Moon, you prove the sun is still around.
I see in you his light still beaming on,
And so, though you're much smaller
And have no light of your own,
Your silver shine is a promise of golden dawn.
Your light still draws me toward you,
You bring brightness to my night.
It's weak but better far than total black.
I hang on to your glimmer; it's the closest thing
I've got to the light I'll have
'Till Brother Sun comes back.

Her assurance had been quickly shattered by the impact of one man. When Lisa began to pick up the fragments around her, she discovered they no longer fit; she had outgrown them. Now she realized her life had no meaning without Jesus Christ as the center.

O Son of God, I look up to You;
You hang so cruelly on that tree.

How could You have gone so far to prove
You could love a child like me?
With Your life You daily show me the way.
Warm, Your love that burns within,
And though Your light was hidden
In the grave three days,
You'll shine forever, for You rose again.

Her voice swelled and rose as Lisa made this promise.
Now her life had meaning and purpose.

And like the moon I prove the Son is still around.
I hope you can from me His message learn.
And though my life is short and I'm nothing on
      my own,
I'm still a living promise of His return.
I'm a mirror of the brightness of the Son.
I'll shine like a living promise until He comes—

Softly, fading away, she ended, "May they see in me
the brightness of Your Son."

When Lisa finished the song and was planning the
next number during the three-minute interlude, Jerome
Thames, after a quick consultation with the others,
stood up. "That's enough, Miss Beall. Thank you.
Would you wait in the next room, please. We'll be with
you in a moment."

Stunned and worried, Lisa knew they hadn't liked
her; she was sure of it. She refused to let them come in
and find her crying, so Lisa sat there as if frozen, not
feeling, not allowing herself to think.

It seemed like eons—it was only seconds—before the
door burst open and Jerome Thames was shaking her
hand, pulling her to her feet in a hug, praising her voice,
a fantastic song, a thrilling performance.

Two of the men were producers for the Christian Broadcasting Corporation, and both added their compliments to his, discussing future dates, an interview, and productions with abandon. The third man, short, plump, with round shining face and red bald spot, was introduced as Walter Wilcox, director of New Song Records, the fastest growing recording company of religious music in the United States.

"Delightful, my dear!" Taking her hand he exclaimed, "Simply delightful. I'd like to offer you a contract and recommend someone as your promoter."

"Oh, but—"

"I realize this is short notice, so I'll just give you these forms, and you can look them over. Talk to your parents and a lawyer." He smiled reassuringly.

"I—" But Lisa never really said anything after that. The men talked on and on around her as she stood by trying to believe this was happening.

On the flight home she pulled out the papers Mr. Wilcox had given her. Just holding them in her hand brought shivers to her spine. The flight attendants were serving soft drinks when Lisa finally took time to look around at her fellow passengers. Across the aisle in front of her sat an older woman who seemed familiar. As if aware of Lisa's eyes on her the woman glanced around. Recognition flickered across her face just as Lisa put a name to her—Inez, the companion to Mark's mother.

Instead of turning back around Inez stared at Lisa, so Lisa felt required to smile. "Hello there, how are you?"

"Okay."

The word was automatic but there was an appeal in Inez's eyes that made Lisa suggest, "Why don't you move back here beside me so we can pass the flight together?"

"I...don't know." Inez shook her head negatively but began to gather up her purse, scarf and magazine.

"Was your trip business or pleasure?" Lisa decided she would do her best to cheer up Inez. She felt so bubbly she wanted everyone to feel the same.

Tears began to trickle down the older woman's face. "I simply don't know what to do. He won't listen to me. Nothing I say—" Abruptly she covered her face with her hands.

Lisa wished she had never looked up. What could she do with this hysterical woman? But she handed Inez a tissue and tried to console her.

Gradually the whole story came out. "Phil...my nephew. He is mixed up with a bad group and—gambles. Now he owes large amounts of money." She sighed.

Lisa tried to remember if she had ever met this young man but didn't think so. She had forgotten all about stumbling upon Inez's secretive conversation with a young man earlier that summer.

"I asked the attorney of my brother's estate if there was any way we could get enough money to pay off the debts, but it would require a lot of legal work which costs money, too. Oh, I don't know what to do." She sat limply in her seat like a sad grey mouse.

"Didn't the lawyer have any suggestion?"

"He said the best thing for Phil would be to admit his guilt and give evidence against the others." She shook her head. "But I already suggested that to Phil, and he refused. He said, 'She's crazy! She'd have me killed!' "

For a moment Lisa thought Phil's problem might have some bearing on José and Mark. But the reference to a woman's involvement confused her. Anyway, Mark was the person to help Inez. He was always helping teens in trouble. "Have you told Mark?"

Inez drew back shrinking into her seat. "No, no. I couldn't." She swallowed trying to regain control of herself. "Mark has been too good to me already."

"But Mark is just the one to help."

"*No.*"

Inez sat up straighter and her lips compressed together. Lisa could tell she was trying to be firm in her refusal. Poor woman, she had been hurt so many times she couldn't believe in herself. By the time they circled the Three Rocks Airport, all Lisa had managed was for Inez to "think about consulting Mark."

Just as the wheels touched the ground Inez gripped Lisa's hand. "Oh, you won't tell Mark, will you? I should never—I told you in confidence." Her chin wobbled. "You won't—"

Inez wouldn't release Lisa until she promised not to tell Mark. *Inez doesn't know that Mark avoids me like the plague,* Lisa thought ruefully and finally agreed. Hoping to help Inez get enough backbone to confront her nephew, Lisa sternly warned her, "Phil might be killed anyway, if the situation is as desperate as you say."

The woman in charge of the wedding arrangements was lining everyone up for the rehearsal when Lisa and Jewel arrived. Kim stood in the foyer with her bridesmaids, who giggled and whispered, anticipating their cue. Randal, standing with Mark and the groomsmen, was at a side door preparing to walk down the side aisle.

"Start the music." The woman called the order to the chorus in an alcove near the front.

As Lisa helped Jewel to a seat at the back of the auditorium, she heard Randal's stage whisper to Mark: "So right after this thing we go check out that truck I saw on my way in."

Mark was to escort Kim, representing their late father. He nodded quickly as Randal and his groomsmen went to their places. Lisa hurried to join the chorus.

"Good. You're here." The director handed Lisa the sheet music. She sang along with the others until time for her solo during the ceremony.

The chorus was singing the wedding march when Kim said, "We have to do it again. I want it paced slowly."

The choral director stuck his head around the corner. "And we need to know exactly how many times to go through it before the bride enters."

"Lisa!" Kim looked past the director. "Will you please be my stand-in while I direct the traffic?" Lisa found herself in the foyer with a distantly polite Mark and the bridesmaids. As she paced slowly down the aisle on Mark's arm, feeling his beating pulse, his strength beside her, Lisa had to concentrate with all her might on keeping her legs upright beneath her black peasant skirt. Setting her face, she rigidly performed the ritual over and over until Kim was satisfied.

Finally the real bride called a halt. "Dinner for everyone at the Homestead! It wouldn't do to keep Flora waiting."

With a sigh of relief Lisa returned to Jewel and helped her into their car. "It's going to be lovely." Jewel settled her purse in her lap and wound a gossamer scarf around her neck. "Randal does seem such a nice young man."

Agreeing, Lisa shut Jewel's door and went around to the driver's side.

"I'm so thankful for Kim's sake she has found such a good man. With Mark as her example I was afraid she might never discover anyone to suit her. He makes most men seem inadequate."

Not about to be drawn out on the subject of Mark

London, Lisa only mumbled, "Hmmm," and concentrated on driving.

Preparing its usual extravagant New Mexico sunset, the whole western sky was a blaze of color. Its beauty made a lump in Lisa's throat, but all things considered, not much was required to form a lump there these days.

Flora had outdone herself. Because so many people were included in the rehearsal dinner a gigantic buffet was laid out. While Jewel filled her plate Lisa got her a drink and located a comfortable spot for her, then filled her own plate.

"I can't understand," Jewel grumbled, "why you insist on keeping your trip to Albuquerque a secret. I want to shout it to everyone I see." She poked her fork through the food on her plate deciding what to eat first.

"Shhhh." Lisa glanced to see who might have heard. Because of a hearing loss Jewel sometimes spoke louder than she realized. "I don't want to take attention away from Kim and Randal." Lisa leaned toward Jewel speaking softly yet distinctly. "Later when I have the contract signed and in my hand, we can announce it. You promised, remember."

Jewel sighed. "It's such a strain. Only another grandmother would appreciate what I'm going through not being able to brag." Sampling a piece of fried chicken she asked, "Do you see Kim? I want to speak to her."

Searching through the throng Lisa first spotted Mark, talking to Randal. His tall commanding person would be difficult to overlook. Kim, standing by, didn't look happy with the discussion. Finally the two men turned decisively and left Kim. Looking frustrated, Kim stood there a moment watching them depart.

Lisa called to her, "Kim, over here."

Kim seemed relieved and hurried toward them. Lisa caught a glimpse of Flora standing at the door behind

Kim. The expression of hate that pursued Kim across the lawn startled Lisa, causing her to wonder about the woman. Resolutely wiping her hands on her apron, Flora went back inside. Suddenly afraid, Lisa rushed to meet Kim and gripped her arm.

"What were you talking about with Randal and Mark?"

"Lisa, what's wrong? I—"

Pulling Kim along Lisa walked toward the back door. "Why did Randal and Mark leave?"

"Oh those two!" Kim tried to break free, dismissing the subject. "I must visit with the guests. It's bad enough for Randal and Mark to desert me; I can't be so rude."

Lisa turned Kim to face her. "Kim, where were they going?" With a small shake of exasperation she said, "Something's up and they may be in danger. Now, tell me!"

"Oh, all right." Kim cocked her head belligerently. "When Randal flew in this afternoon he saw a semi-truck parked at the old homestead. Because of the gun shots that day we rode out, they thought they had to investigate right now—" Her voice broke betraying her hurt. "Our rehearsal dinner!" Clearing her throat she laughed. "*Men*!"

Lisa had gone white, and her hand on Kim became cold. "Lisa, what's wrong?"

"I don't know." Lisa's mind whirled with possibilities. Most of all she remembered Inez's distress, her saying, "*She's* crazy!" This connected with the icy blue anger in Flora's eyes. Once again yanking Kim along Lisa headed for the kitchen door. "But I think I know someone who does."

Finally feeling some concern, Kim followed. When Lisa put a finger to her lips as they carefully crossed the threshold, she stopped her questions so Flora didn't hear them enter.

Her attention was concentrated on the citizen's band radio. Speaking rapid Spanish, Flora tried to make contact with someone.

The static was terrible, so the receiver kept asking her to repeat the message. Even in another language, it was clear to Kim and Lisa that she was warning someone that Mark and Randal were on their way to the old homestead.

A piercing wail of static gave Lisa the impetus to leap across the room and knock the hand microphone from Flora's hand. Rapidly Lisa searched for the power switch and flipped it off. Instead of fleeing as Lisa thought she might, Flora lunged at her, sending Lisa reeling backwards.

In one motion, Flora had the power back on and was screaming orders. Twirling the dials Lisa clutched Flora's arm, trying to throw her to the floor. Finally Kim entered the fray. The two women subdued Flora, pinning her to the floor.

"What's this all about?" Kim, having no time to worry about decorum, sat astride the older woman.

Before answering, Lisa once again switched off the power. "There!" Grimacing with satisfaction she joined Kim. "I only know Mark and Randal are in danger, especially if her message got through."

Fire blazed for a moment in Flora's blue eyes; then they narrowed craftily. Indignantly she demanded, "What is the meaning of this? I have much to do for the dinner." She tried to sit up.

"What are we going to do with her?"

"Let me think. Since we don't know enough to call the police, all we can do is keep her here until Mark and Randal return."

Inez entered the kitchen. "Kim!" she gasped. "What's going on?" Seeing the woman beneath Kim and Lisa, Inez stared amazed. "Flora!" Then a smile of pleasure played across her face. "Good."

Her satisfaction at seeing Flora sprawled on the floor made another piece come into place for Lisa. "Where's your nephew?"

"I don't know, but something about tonight has him as nervous as can be."

"Flora was trying to warn someone on the radio, but Lisa stopped her."

"Inez, you sit on Flora's feet while Kim finds something to tie her up." Lisa shifted her weight as Kim stood up. To Inez she said, "You do realize that Phil might be picked up when we call the police?"

"It's gone too far now." Inez spoke firmly, her jawline tightening. "She's not going to threaten Phil or me any longer."

"She threatened you?"

"Not in so many words, but insinuations all the time. Frightening me and smiling nasty-like." When Flora filled the air with Spanish-English profanity and tried to kick free, Inez pressed harder on her, enjoying the role of conqueror.

"Can you guard her, Inez, because Kim must return to her guests?"

"Gladly." Inez's face glowed with satisfaction.

Tying Flora with some long-forgotten clothesline, they moved her to Inez's room where no one would likely pop in on them. Then Kim and Lisa smoothed their hair, and taking deep breaths, returned to the patio.

"There you are, Kim." Immediately she was caught up in a crowd of people.

Slowly Lisa joined Jewel. The most difficult thing she

162

had ever done in her whole life, she decided, was to return to the party instead of following Randal…and Mark.

As he drove the four-wheel-drive pickup the long way around the pastures, Mark wondered where José could be. How had the young man finally managed to elude his watchful eye?

Interrupting Mark's thoughts, Randal asked, "You feel this semi might be a hijacked liquor truck?"

"When I called the police earlier, they said another hijacking was reported tonight." The day of the horseback ride they had found large tire tracks, cigarette butts, and beer cans. Mark now thought the crew had enjoyed a break before completing their task.

"Any ideas who's the ramrod?" Randal readjusted the visor to block out the last glare of the setting sun.

"Since they're using my ranch, I figure it's someone out here." Mark twisted the steering wheel to dodge a mesquite tree. "I'm usually traveling, but this summer I changed my plans."

"So it has to be someone in your household?"

"I'm afraid so." With the sun gone, Mark slowed the pickup. "My aide in Santa Fe knows when I breathe, but political deviousness is his meat—not hijackings."

"And you can eliminate Kim and your mother." Randal mentally reviewed the household members he'd met.

"And Inez." But as Mark added her name he remembered her problems with Phil earlier. No, she didn't have the strength of character to mastermind anything. She might, however, be someone's tool.

Randal had caught his hesitation. "Maybe Inez and her nephew?"

"Why do you mention him?" Mark glanced at Randal, whose face was barely visible in the cab.

"Tried to appear a wheeler-dealer when I met him." His voice expressed his distaste.

"I don't think he could be in charge, do you?"

"Nope. Phil is a peon. Someone else does the thinking."

Mark tried to consider other possibilities. Like maybe his foreman, Lee? Somehow Lee didn't fit.

A three-quarter moon rose but hardly made any impression on the landscape. Mark had to shift down to a crawl because turning on the lights might warn those at the old house. Finally a half-mile from the ranch house they left the pickup and began to walk. Mark stuck a flashlight in his back pocket as a precaution. When they crept near to the large barn, a shaded lantern showed someone transferring cases from the semi to an unmarked truck. As the man stooped to pick up another case, the light shone on his face. Phil.

More angry than surprised Mark stood up and knocked a rake over. Randal grabbed for it but the tool clattered across the wood before hitting the dirt. The noise made Phil freeze; then he bolted for the wide front door. Cursing himself for his carelessness Mark kicked the rake out of the way and entered the small side door.

Following, Randal whispered, "I get one point for being right about Phil."

Quickly they noted license plates and merchandise for fear Phil would return with reinforcements. Then Mark gestured toward the house. "I'll try to keep my feet out of trouble this time."

"Right." Randal grinned at Mark's quiet remark. Joking seemed to make it all a little easier. "Now why do they hijack this stuff?" They waited behind some barrels in front of the barn to see if anything moved.

"This brand can't be purchased on the east coast except in the black market."

"Must be great money." A low sigh of humorous envy came from Randal.

Mark peeked over the barrel rim and motioned Randal to move. "Some like the thrill and planning more."

Reaching the side of the house without incident, they wondered what had become of Phil. They had almost circled the house when Randal put out a hand to stop Mark. A sliver of light shone beside a drawn blind just inside the old screened-in porch. Hearing nothing, they poised to enter when the sound of static came to them.

The static was so bad they couldn't understand anything, but it did make a cover noise, so they tiptoed across the old boards on the porch. Reaching the window they crouched beneath it, letting out a long breath they had held from the moment of opening the old screen door. Only more static rewarded their patience. Mark rose to enter the house.

At that moment, a door opened and a voice said, "I don't know why Carlos puts up with you." A chair was pulled back, and the static came and went as the dials on the radio were adjusted.

"But I heard—" Phil's voice revealed him as the object of the other's anger.

"You *say* you heard. And when we go investigate we find nothing." More noises, then the man said, "Come in, Big Mama, come in." There was no response. "I had Flora earlier, but the transmission was garbled, now I can't raise her." His attention returned to Phil. "Get back out there and shift those cases. It's going to take us all night since José disappeared."

"José was smart," Phil muttered rebelliously, before shuffling out.

Mark motioned to Randal to retreat. They had heard

165

enough. Slowly they made their way across the old boards until finally they were out the door and off the porch. There they discussed their strategy.

"Let's jump 'em, while they're separated," suggested Randal. "Then we can either wait for this Carlos guy or go tackle Flora."

"Flora and her CB." Mark shook his head in disgust that he hadn't thought of her sooner.

"You know this Carlos?"

"I know Carlos well." Mark compressed his mouth in concentration. "Phil will be easy to handle; let's take the guy in here first. I figure he's one of the birds who jumped José and me one night. All the pieces are beginning to fit."

"Yes, aren't they." A clicking of a trigger accompanied the smirking voice. "Don't move, Mark." He came around them slowly. "And the happy bridegroom, I see."

"Carlos?" Randal raised an eyebrow at Mark.

"Right the first time." Gesturing with the small gun in his hand Carl ordered, "Hands high." To the man with him he instructed, "Check them."

The burly Mexican quickly ran his hands over their length. "*Nada.*"

"To the barn. It will seem you have had a quarrel over the goods when they find you."

As they walked to the barn, Mark knew he should try to get Carl to talk, but he couldn't bring himself to speak. Carl Valdez was a part of the past he had tried to blot out. Yet here they were again, their lives entwined.

A commotion from within the house stopped them. With Carl's attention momentarily deflected, Mark and Randal attacked together. Randal tackled him and Mark knocked the gun from Carl's hand.

Carl had Mark down by the throat, strangling him.

Hazily Mark seemed to be reliving the time Carl attacked him after he'd run down Roberta Valdez.

Recalling that time made Mark suddenly go slack. Beneath Carl, Mark ceased to struggle. Perhaps he should let Carl kill him as just retribution. Then his feeling of guilt would be vanquished forever.

At Mark's stillness, Carl loosened his grip and searched for the gun. Then with a supreme effort Mark threw Carl off, kicking him solidly and picking up the gun.

While Carl writhed in the dirt, Mark called to Randal, "I've got the gun."

"And he's—got a—knife." Randal gasped the words as he fought.

Afraid to shoot, Mark hesitated. A wiry figure burst from the house. José! Sizing up the situation José entered the contest between Randal and the thug. Taking hold of the hand wielding the knife José forced him to drop it.

"The barn," directed José. "Phil is there, and rope."

"What about the CB operator?" Mark jerked Carl to his feet.

"Tied to a chair, Mr. Mark." José helped Randal stand and used the knife to coerce Carl.

"How did you get here?" Mark's head throbbed. The old concussion hadn't been ready for this pounding.

José stood tall with hurt dignity. "You know I watch over you. *Señora* Beall, *mi* Dulce, Miss Lisa—they would never forgive me if something happened to you."

Lisa? Would she care? But Mark didn't have time to conjecture on that. "To the barn." Mimicking Carl's gesture, he waved the gun at the two men.

Randal fell in beside Mark and José. "José, that still doesn't explain how you got out here."

José grinned. "In the back of the pickup, of course."

Their laughter made Phil turn around. When he saw Carl and his henchman followed by the other three men he began to whine. "José, you know I didn't want to do this. They made me."

"Quiet, Phil." Mark rubbed his head. No wonder Inez was at her wit's end. After Randal and José trussed up Carl and his accomplice, they had a conference.

"I called the police on the CB." José hesitated. "It was the only thing to do." He shrugged in resignation. "My punishment will be nothing compared to my joy at seeing that pig—" He thumbed rudely at Carl.

José looked down on Carl hunched over in the dirt. "Many years ago I vowed upon the body of my dead sister I would revenge his murder of her. Then I was a boy and could do nothing. Now I am a man, and it is done."

"Murder?" Mark laid a hand on José's shoulder in consternation. "No, José. I killed your sister. I ran her down with my car. Not Carl."

José looked up at Mark in pity. "Is that what you've believed all these years, my friend? You were only the instrument. This *hombre malísimo*—" He glanced bitterly at Carlos. "He planned the accident to collect the insurance on her life. Purposely he ran her into the street. Roberta, she was running in fear of her life."

Then tears began to fill the dark eyes, José's hands trembling at his side until he clenched them tight. "*Mi Roberta, mi hermosa*, my lovely sister, Roberta."

"How does she figure in?" Randal was still amazed that the housekeeper was involved.

"Flora, she is Carlos's mother." To José this answered all the questions. "They're of the same thought."

José waited in front of the main house for the police to finish at the old ranch and come. Randal and Mark split up to find Flora, but Randal spotted Kim and forgot anything else for some time.

Mark dusted off his summer sweater and brushed back a lock of brown hair before approaching Jewel, who sat beneath a tree, yard lanterns illuminating the area. Just as Mark reached Jewel's side Lisa rushed over, her brow furrowed.

"Mark!" She clutched his arm and pulled him toward the house. "I, we need you."

"What's the problem?"

As she drew Mark into the kitchen, Lisa glanced quickly around to make sure they couldn't be overheard. "It's about Flora."

"Flora!" Mark stopped in his tracks. "Where is she?"

"Kim and I, with Inez's help—" She stopped, feeling extremely foolish. "We tied her up. Inez is watching her up in her room."

"You did what?" Mark took her trembling hands in his and drew Lisa closer. Knowing that Flora was out of commission, Mark held her firmly and studied her features. It had been too long since she had been in his arms.

"Well," Lisa tugged to remove her hands but Mark ignored her. She tried to forget her erratic pulse and explain. "She was warning someone on the CB that you and Randal were on your way to the ranch house so—"

Mark threw back his head and laughed. "So you and Kim tackled her and tied her up?"

"Exactly." Lisa smiled, her dimple showing.

It was more than Mark could resist. He folded Lisa into his arms and kissed her eagerly.

She had meant to tell him about Inez and Phil, but she forgot everything with his kiss, yielding to his intensity and giving in return. For moments the world was forgotten in their embrace; then Mark withdrew slowly.

Breathing deeply he said, "I came after Flora."

"She's with Inez." Lisa leaned against the wall as he passed her on the stairs.

"I know the way."

Lisa nodded brusquely and returned to the garden. There she met Kim and learned enough bits of the story to feel she could take Jewel home and come back to hear more when the men returned from the police station.

After the guests left, the women gravitated to the patio, finding comfortable spots to put up their feet or nibble on the food still spread out on the tables.

Busy playing the hostess to Randal's parents, Edwina hadn't missed Flora until now.

"Inez." She tried to keep her voice low. "Where's Flora? Surely she isn't pouting, just when I need her most."

Not certain what to say until Mark arrived, Inez offered, "What is it you need? I'll be glad to help."

"Could you take Randal's parents up to their room? I'm exhausted."

"Of course." Inez was glad to have something to do. It made the time pass more swiftly.

After Inez escorted Mr. and Mrs. Moore inside, Edwina surveyed the others. Kim and Lisa had plates and were eating for the first time that evening. Randal was at the buffet piling a plate high.

"Where's your brother?" She sighed as if she carried the world. "You all vanish when you're needed. Doesn't Mark realize this wedding requires everyone's cooperation?"

"Sit down, Edwina." Kim kicked her shoes off and padded across to guide her mother to the large fan chair. "I'll get you some coffee."

Appreciating this solicitude, Edwina smiled wanly.

"You probably haven't eaten, either."

"When would I have had time?"

Kim pulled over a wicker footstool and propped Edwina's feet on it. "There. I'll get you some food."

"Thank you, dear." Kim's attention had sidetracked her from Mark. "Everything went well. There are a few things about the ceremony that have me worried." She accepted the plate from Kim. "If it were my wedding, I'd have more flowers and candles for every pew. After all, our friends will expect you to have the best of everything."

Since Randal and Lisa weren't helping her, and Inez, who had returned, never said anything, Kim tried to keep her mother going. "I think it's lovely. You've done so much."

"I want it to be perfect."

Mark entered with Phil and José beside him. They were behind Inez and Edwina, who went on about the wedding. "I want your wedding to be marvelous, exciting. Nothing exciting ever happens here!" She spread her hands in a dramatic gesture.

At that moment Lisa's eyes met Mark's tawny-gold ones. Smiling across the expanse of room, they shared the intimacy of several recent adventures. Seeing Lisa smile, Inez glanced around and caught sight of Mark, Phil, and José. She stood so rapidly, she dropped her needlepoint. Crossing to her nephew she took him in her arms where he cried like a baby. They went up to her room.

At this Edwina, amazed, demanded, "What on earth is happening?" As her eyes went round the group she beheld such looks of innocence that she pointed at Kim and said, "Kim, what have you been up to?"

She couldn't be certain, but Lisa thought Kim was the first to snicker, then Randal. Mark and Lisa joined in, tears of laughter streaming down their faces. Feeling indignant Edwina endured this display with a stony face.

"We're not laughing at you, Mother." Mark pulled up a chair beside her and patted her hand until they could all regain their composure. "It's just that there has been something happening. You're right about that."

Still a little huffy Edwina said, "Explain, please."

"Explain everything!" Kim snuggled closer to Randal on the couch.

"Begin with Phil," suggested Randal.

Lisa realized then that José, looking worn out, had slipped away during their laughter.

"I can't start with Phil. Carl and Flora are the beginning."

"Flora!" Edwina set down her cup. "Where is she?"

"In jail."

Edwina, forgetting herself, let her jaw drop. Recovering she said, "Well, explain!"

"Carl, assisted by Flora, dabbled in numerous unsavory activities. Phil was caught in their nets by gambling. Hijacking beer to sell in unfranchised area black markets is the latest of their dealings. José worked for reasons of his own, but he was picked up on a DWI charge and had to take my class. That put a kink in the works."

"Plus," commented Kim, "you promised me to stay here this summer. No wonder Flora was cranky."

"So Carl sent his men to put me out of commission. But José was with me that night and helped me. So his life was on the line for me."

"But that doesn't explain some other things like the pendant and the window peeper. Are they connected?" Kim looked at her mother, then Lisa, before returning to Mark.

"That's where Phil comes in. He took the pendant for

172

some money, and he was the prowler. He was also the one who burglarized The Bells."

"What happens to him?" Since her visit with Inez on the plane, Lisa felt sorry for her.

"He will testify and plea-bargain." Mark went to the buffet. "And so will José." He picked up a plate. "I'm starved. Has everyone else eaten?"

Edwina stood up. Exhausted, she looked at the buffet like a bewildered child, at the plates and glasses scattered around.

Kim pulled Randal to his feet. "Go on to bed, Mother. We'll clean up the mess." She took the plate from Edwina and pointed her toward the stairs.

Lisa carried some dishes into the kitchen. It wasn't long before they had the mess all cleaned away and the dishwasher loaded. Lisa slipped away while Mark and Randal were on the patio folding up the tables and chairs.

When she reached her car out front, Lisa discovered José asleep in the front seat. When she opened her door he woke up and looked sheepish.

"I was so tired, I thought...if I could catch a ride?"

"I'm glad you did." His company would keep her from trying to define the meaning of that intense kiss on the stairway.

Chapter Twelve

The day for Kim's wedding had finally arrived. Lisa sipped her orange juice and thought of last night. Mark's kiss, of course, was unforgettable. But what sent chills up her spine was the memory of his slow smile and the look they shared at Edwina's statement that "Nothing ever happens."

Jewel picked up her coffee cup and refilled it with decaffeinated. "Kim's wedding day." She shook her head. "It's difficult to realize that she's old enough. I can remember…"

Shamelessly Lisa encouraged Jewel to talk on. When the meal was completed, they moved to the porch and snapped green beans. Lisa listened eagerly to every word Jewel could recall about the two children she'd watched over like a guardian angel as they grew.

"And there was the time Mark and Kim knocked on my back door and stood there, eyes wide and hands behind their backs. 'What have you got?' I asked. Proudly they brought forth a bunch of wilting desert flowers in a paper basket that read, We Love You. Happy Mother's Day." Jewel wiped her eyes. "I could have wept, they were so sweet."

Memories, thought Lisa. *No one can take memories*

from you. While Jewel rambled on weaving a spell of nostalgia Lisa knew she would treasure her memories, too. When she closed her eyes she could see Mark—supporting her as she sang; pausing to glory in the beauty of a desert flower; laughing in joy, his head thrown back; his jaw firming implacably as he expressed his views; and always that slow, crooked smile accented by glinting hazel eyes.

Kim was dressing at the church to prevent crushing her wedding dress on the way. So Lisa and Jewel had been asked to arrive early to help her change. Lisa opened the door to the class room Kim was using. Edwina was next door helping the bridesmaids, and Kim was reading from her New Testament. "Come in. Jewel, I'm so glad you're here." Kim hugged Jewel tightly and nearly knocked off the lavender hat that coordinated with Jewel's print dress of lavender, pink, and gray.

Then Kim looked at Lisa. "My! You are glowing in that lemon yellow." She squeezed her hand. "You're not supposed to outshine the bride."

Lisa laughed, accepting the compliment. She knew the color was good on her, and the halo of white daisies entwined in her hair gave her an ethereal quality. "Silly. There's no way, not today. Love wins the beauty contest every time."

"Do I look okay?" Kim turned slowly before them. Her hair shone, each strand in place. Her makeup was light, her nails were buffed, and light fragrance scented the air when she moved.

"Simply gorgeous." Lisa lifted the wedding dress and admired the cutwork around the high neckline. "Are you ready to put this on?"

"As soon as Mother comes back."

"I'll go get a good seat in the auditorium," said Jewel.

"You're not going to stay?" Kim looked up from pointing out the handwork on the gown to Lisa. "I wanted you in some of the pictures."

As she spoke the classroom door clicked, and the three women turned to see Edwina leaning against the closed door. Lisa knew she was ridiculous, but she felt as if she'd been caught in a guilty secret.

Jewel's grip tightened on her clutch bag. "Edwina. You're a beautiful bride, Kim. I'll leave you now." She moved slowly toward the door.

Neither Kim nor Lisa could think of anything to say. Then Lisa quickly joined Jewel to help support her. They were halfway across the room, the silence tense, when Edwina finally spoke. "The photographer is here." She managed a smile. "Why don't you have a picture taken with Kim before you go?"

Jewel's eyes lit up. "Thank you, Edwina, I will."

Lisa picked up the wedding dress and lifted it high so that Kim could let it slide down without messing up her hair. Then Lisa began to button up the back.

At a knock on the door, Edwina opened it to let in the bridesmaids and the photographer. He took a picture of Lisa doing up the buttons, then one with Kim and Jewel together, and one of Jewel, Kim and Lisa. While Lisa helped Jewel to the auditorium he posed the others, taking shot after shot.

When she returned, Lisa heard one of the bridesmaids complain, "This is taking longer than the ceremony will."

"But all this," another girl responded, "only happens once in your life."

"And I'm a sentimentalist," Kim put in, "so smile. It will soon be over."

Lisa was included in several more pictures before she went to join the chorus.

"Let's go over this song one more time. We don't hold this measure long enough." Their director was having last-minute fidgets. "Everyone keep your eyes on me." He hummed the pitch and gave the signal to begin.

When he was satisfied, they left the practice room and entered the alcove where they would stand during the wedding.

From where they stood only one of the chorus members could see what was happening, and she reported in a whisper, "The church is packed." She peered around the corner. "Here come the candlelighters."

The two young men came up on the platform to light the candles, so the chorus could see this. White daisies and yellow bows were everywhere.

"They're bringing in Randal's parents." She waited. "Now Mrs. London is coming down the aisle." The chorus members cleared their throats. It was time to sing. They sang several love songs, then a hush fell over the audience. The bridesmaids stood at the back door. Led by Randal the groomsmen took their places. Then the traditional "Faithful and True" swelled forth.

As the chorus entered the final segment of the march, emphasizing each word, Kim and Mark paced regally down the long aisle. Radiant, lovely, suddenly shy, she approached the altar. Randal's whole being was riveted on Kim. As each step brought her closer to him he soaked in her joyous love of life and her fresh beauty.

Lisa was so glad they could see the platform from where they stood. Randal's love and admiration shone in his eyes. How wonderful that these two good people had found each other. Lisa rejoiced in their happiness. Yet her own heart ached because she hadn't opened her eyes, nor her mind, until too late.

As soon as Mark placed Kim's hand in Randal's, Lisa stepped forward for her solo, "The Wedding Song."

But Mark, instead of joining his mother as Lisa expected, walked toward her, past the flower girl, past the bridesmaids. Their dresses rustled to let him through. He stopped beside Lisa.

The choral director blew softly on his pitch pipe. Lisa knew it was time for her to sing, but she felt faint. What was Mark doing? She swayed slightly, her color gone. Then Mark had his hand beneath her elbow, firmly supporting her. Taking a deep breath, Lisa produced the first words of the song.

Afterward Mark sang "Hand in Hand," his tenor clear and true. He still held her hand, and often his eyes rested on Lisa. Finally Mark left her side and Lisa stepped back into the alcove. She tried to concentrate on the ceremony, but she could only feel his hand on hers and envision his glinting eyes looking deep into her soul. Could he have meant any of what he sang? Lisa couldn't relinquish this hope.

When the receiving line broke up, Ann Nix, from the newspaper, motioned to Lisa. "Over here!"

Lisa balanced her cake and punch and joined Ann's group. She reminded herself on the way to be careful what she said to Ann. The woman had a way of making you talk.

"Lisa! You were marvelous!"

"Thank you." Lisa smiled as others seconded Ann's praise. "It's a beautiful wedding."

"The event of the year!" said one.

But Ann shook her head. "You must not have seen tonight's paper. Carl Valdez is the biggest news in a long time."

"What do you mean?"

Ann had their attention now. "He masterminded those hijackings of beer trucks all over the state. And he didn't stop at murder."

Lisa kept quiet and ate her cake, glad to rest a minute.

Soon they exhausted that subject so Ann turned back to Lisa. "What are your plans when summer is over? About singing, I mean."

"You sang on George Mahon's show, didn't you? You were wonderful!"

"I remember now. You were super!"

"I'd like to hear you do more," suggested another. "Kim!" She waved her hand to attract the bride's attention.

Seeing Lisa and Ann, Kim immediately began to thread her way through the crowd. The woman didn't wait, instead calling across the room. "Kim, we want Lisa to sing some more right now."

"Oh no, not here." Lisa shook her head and tried to shush the instigator. But the idea grew and it became impossible to refuse politely. Frantically Lisa wondered what to sing. Catching Mark watching her, Lisa suddenly knew. She would sing her song. Perhaps he would understand the message of her heart.

O Sun I look up to you,
You hang so peacefully in the sky—

The crowd gathered around to get a better view, and Lisa lost sight of Mark.

When the song ended Kim whispered under cover of the applause, "It's time to change into my traveling suit. Will you help me?"

"I'd love to," Lisa whispered back. But she was delayed by well-wishers. Automatically responding, Lisa

179

thought of Kim's leaving. Kim had been a good friend to her all summer. They had talked for hours, played tennis, and shopped.

When Lisa first came to live with Jewel she had expected long, lonely solitude. Lisa had learned much from Jewel, but she was glad the summer had included Kim too.

As she shut the door to the changing room, Lisa wiped at her eyes. One of the bridesmaids surreptitiously handed her several net bags of rice tied up with little yellow ribbons. "You'll want some to throw." She giggled and continued to pass them out while Kim slipped out of her wedding gown.

First handing her the mint green skirt, a bridesmaid asked, "Where are you going?"

Kim pulled it on and buttoned the waist. "To Ruidosa. Inn of the Mountain Gods."

"What's it like?" Lisa felt the conversation must be kept light or she was going to dissolve into tears.

Finally Kim was dressed, the last suitcase closed, the makeup bag secure. Everyone fell silent. This was the final moment of the ceremony. This parting made the vows and all they included emphatically real.

Now the tears came as Kim hugged each one. At last, as she reached Lisa, words wouldn't come. They held each other mutely, tightly. Lisa heard Kim softly whisper, struggling with emotion, "Oh, Lisa, how I wish...I don't know what went wrong..."

"I know," soothed Lisa, "Shhh."

The door opened and they all crowded into the hallway where Randal waited to escort Kim.

"Throw the bouquet!"

Turning her back Kim tossed the flowers over her shoulder. As the bouquet of fragrant yellow and white blossoms arched in the air, Lisa melted into the group, the others surging forward. She never knew who caught it.

"I'm going straight to bed." Lisa rubbed her neck muscles with one hand as she drove.

Jewel removed her glasses and pretended to clean them while actually wiping away tears. "It has been a tiring day."

Aware of her grandmother's subterfuge Lisa smiled in the semi-darkness of the car. "A lovely wedding, wasn't it?"

"Lovely, lovely." Jewel made a good job of drying her eyes. "I keep remembering special moments and start crying all over again."

Lisa remembered special moments, too.

"We're home!" announced the older woman as Lisa stopped in the driveway. Jewel leaned gratefully on her arm, glad that Lisa wasn't inclined to chatter. She didn't remember being this emotionally exhausted after her own children's marriages. As they entered her bedroom Jewel studied Lisa's face in the light. The little-girl-lost look in her granddaughter's eyes probably accounted more than anything for her tiredness. Jewel longed to be able to kiss the hurt and make it go away, but she sensed Lisa's emotions were too delicate for intrusion. She sighed.

"Are you okay?" Lisa looked up from the bureau where she was getting out Jewel's nightgown.

"Fine. Only tired." She fluttered her hand at her night things. "Thank you, dear. Now run along to bed."

In her room Lisa feverishly undressed, ripping the yellow dress from her body and flinging it to the floor. Quickly getting into a shortie nightgown she threw herself across the bed and let the tears flow uncontrolled.

How long she cried Lisa didn't know. But she cried

until she was calm. It was a calm born of acceptance, of new determination to live with the consequences of her own bullheadedness and make the best of life. In that decision came the resolve to stay with Jewel, not just for these three months, but for as long as Jewel needed her. She could travel from here to singing engagements and when she was exhausted she could return to Jewel's solid faith and love.

Lisa was in that half-world between waking and sleeping when the telephone rang. She tilted her hand to see her watch. Why, it was only ten o'clock. The wedding had begun at five with the supper reception soon after, but surely more time had elapsed than that. Groping for the receiver in the dark Lisa lifted it to her ear. "Hello-o." Her throat was still clogged from the crying.

"Lisa?" Mark London repeated her name.

She had to gulp for air before she could respond. Even so her yes was more a squeak than a word.

"You're okay?"

At first Lisa nodded at the phone, unable to speak, before realizing her stupidity. "Yes."

He paused. Just to know Mark was on the other end of the line brought her overwhelming joy. Hope burst free, fluttering gossamer wings inside her.

"Lisa." Mark spoke her name again before plunging in. "I have a political rally on Saturday. And a teen outreach on Sunday in Odessa. But Monday night is the dinner ending the Adventures in Living Free class and…" He hesitated only an instant before finishing decisively. "And you're going with me. Monday night at seven. It's formal."

"Yes." Lisa accepted his dictate in a hoarse whisper, tears gathering on her lower lashes.

Again Mark demanded, "Are you okay?"

The silence became tangible. What could she say? She couldn't shout, or laugh, or cry with joy. She couldn't explain anything over a telephone. All she could say was yes once more. But this time it came out firm, confident, "Yes!"

"Goodnight then."

"Yes," whispered Lisa into the silent receiver. "Yes, yes, yes!" Hugging the instrument to her, she let the silly tears fall. *Yes, yes, yes,* sang her heart. A heart full of songs to sing.

Lisa handed the waitress her plate and watched Mark beside her. He pushed back his chair and stood, his hands gripping the lectern before him.

"First, I want to welcome our guests." He smiled and Lisa's heart double-timed. Then he introduced those at the head table.

"This is the final session of our class and we are pleased to have you share it with us." He paused briefly, and Lisa could feel a surge of anticipation from the participants. Slowly his eyes made contact with each one. "You are tonight's program. Tonight you will be telling us the most valuable benefit you've gained from this course." He paused again and took a deep breath. "To get things started I will tell you what I've gained."

Concisely Mark told of how he'd always carried a heavy burden of guilt because he had run down and killed someone. "This changed my life. I dedicated myself to helping others change their lives so they wouldn't wander aimlessly through life day after day."

His glance rested on José. "Then on Friday night I learned through a member of this class that although I was at fault because I was drunk and driving too fast, all the blame wasn't mine."

He caught Lisa's eyes briefly before looking around

183

again. "So I've learned to give thanks for my suffering. If I hadn't lived under this delusion of guilt, I wouldn't be here with you now."

As the applause resounded, Lisa wiped tears from her eyes. She wasn't alone in her emotional response, for there wasn't a dry eye in the house. Then Mark introduced the first student, handed him his certificate, and sat beside Lisa. Unselfconsciously she covered his hand, squeezing it understandingly.

Immediately he looked at her. Slowly he smiled that enchanting crooked smile. Mark grasped her hand securely in both of his out of sight beneath the tablecloth.

These young people had led unhappy lives. They were old and wise in the treachery of the world. Just learning to believe in the goodness and honor of some people was a giant step. Lisa wanted to be a part of this process, assisting Mark as he guided others to help themselves. Though she was an emotional rag when the dinner ended, Lisa also felt uplifted. Tonight she'd witnessed a rare event, a spiritual mountain top she would remember for the rest of her life.

While Mark congratulated his students, José and Dulce made a beeline in Lisa's direction. Protectively shepherding Dulce before him, José guided her through the laughing and crying crowd.

"How are you two this evening?"

"We have an announcement." Dulce hugged close to José.

Widening her eyes in anticipation of their news Lisa wasn't altogether surprised when José took his cue and brusquely said, "Dulce has consented to be my wife."

"Congratulations!" Lisa hugged Dulce enthusiastically. "I'm so happy for you."

When Mark joined them, José had to repeat his good news. "This is great!" Mark wrung his hand and thumped him on the back. "I don't know what your plans are, but I'd like to see you two live on Jewel's place, taking care of her and the grounds. I'll consult her, of course, but it would relieve my mind about her."

Even though she had already come to the same conclusion, Lisa thought this was a little high-handed of Mark. She remained silent only because one of her promises to herself had been to learn to control her temper.

Mark and Lisa were the last to leave. The August moon hung low in the sky. Under the streetlights, the parking lot was almost as bright as day. Lisa leaned against the locked door of the car while Mark put the box of class materials in the trunk. Instead of immediately opening her door Mark also leaned against the car and looked up at the moon, big and orange.

Suddenly panicky, Lisa broke the silence. "Have you heard from Kim and Randal? How are they doing?"

Mark stopped her nervous chatter by placing his hand over hers on the hood and demanding, "Lisa, what happened in Albuquerque?"

Lisa's mind flashed back to her audition. Her eyes lit up; her mouth curved, then thinned in anger. How did Mark know about her trip to Albuquerque? Jerking her hand free Lisa faced him, her long dress swaying around her. "What do you mean?"

"Lisa!" Ruthlessly Mark reclaimed her hand and captured the other so she couldn't escape. "Lisa," he repeated in a gentler tone. "Tell me about your trip. Did you audition? How did it go?"

Fiercely she tried to pull free, but he gripped her until she ceased struggling. "How did you know?" Her chin tilted defiantly. The moonlight sent reflecting sparks from her eyes. "How could you know? I only told Kim and Jewel." Had one of them—?

185

"I took Jerome the videotape of your performance here."

Lisa became very still. "Now why did you do that?" Her demure manner and the cocking of her head to one side deceived Mark into thinking her anger had subsided. So he was caught off guard when she yanked free.

Folding her arms to protect her hands she asked again, "Why did you do that? Can't you leave my life alone? Do you enjoy manipulating others so no one is free of your intervention?"

She probably would have gone on flinging bitter accusations, a release of the pent up tension of the past weeks, but Mark turned away from her. A car circled through the parking lot, spotlighting them as they stood frozen like wax dummies in a dramatic scene. Then Mark hit the hood with his fist and faced her again.

"No, I can't leave your life alone." His voice was ragged. "I love you. I'm sorry you see my efforts as manipulation. I saw them as a last ditch attempt to keep you here. I was afraid you would go away when the summer was over. Much of my work is in Santa Fe and Albuquerque. I hoped with time you might love me." He stood straight and tall before her, his arms at his sides, the flashing yellow in his hazel eyes softened to a vulnerable glow.

Lisa's heart contracted. After all her noble promises to change her life, to control her temper, she had attacked him like a virago. She had realized a change wouldn't be easy, but that she'd have to work at it every hour of every day was overwhelming. Even so, Mark London had said he loved her.

"You do? You did?"

Her soft questions, full of unbelieving wonder, set him free to catch her shoulders, holding her to the spot as he searched the brown depths of her eyes.

Lisa yielded to the pressure of his hands and moved closer. Hesitantly she raised a hand to his cheek, lightly stroking the laugh lines, touching the scar near his temple.

At her caress his fingers tightened, and his breathing quickened. Lisa's heartbeat raced in anticipation. Her skin seemed on fire as their eyes locked, then closed, as his lips met hers.

Hungrily he kissed her as if he must take this offering now for fear it would be as quickly wrenched away. Then his lips softened, tenderly exploring the corners of her mouth, the sensitive skin of her eyelids, the pulse in her throat.

Lisa didn't draw away or struggle. She melted against Mark, responding to his embrace with her own repressed longing of the past weeks. His kisses intensified until she clung weakly in his arms.

Finally, holding her crushed against him and drawing deep, steadying breaths, he asked, "Lisa, will you marry me?"

"Yes." There was no hesitation in Lisa's response. Snuggling into his shoulder she added provocatively, "I thought you'd never ask!"

Lifting her chin with a warm caressing finger, Mark laughed, then brushed her nose. "You haven't given me much of a chance."

He couldn't resist tasting the sweetness of her trembling lips again. After one more tender, lingering kiss, Mark prompted her to answer the question that had started this reconciliation. "How did things go in Albuquerque?"

This time Lisa remained in his arms as she told him of her excitement, then her fears, and ultimately her decision to sing her own song, "Mirror of Brightness."

"The one you sang at the reception?" He twined a

golden curl through his fingers. "I want to hear it again."

Since Lisa hadn't even been certain he'd heard it earlier, he surprised her by adding, "I loved it."

Clasping this small reward as more important than all the world's acclaim, she confessed, "I'm glad you do, but I was still astounded when they offered me a contract."

"You signed a contract?"

"I had already decided I wouldn't rejoin my—the group and tour." She leaned back to see his expression. "I thought this a heaven-sent opportunity to sing and still live with Jewel. Since this seems to be the time for confession, I wanted to be near you too." She blushed at this, but Mark didn't respond, his eyes still waiting for the answer to his question.

"Yes, I signed a contract. I mailed it yesterday." Did he feel she shouldn't work? Would it make a difference to their future? "For the first time since this summer began, I have a direction; I 'know where I'm going.' But I don't know whether I can bear it if you object. Do you?"

Laughing aloud and lifting her off her feet, Mark swung her around. "Object? I want you to sing!"

When once again her feet were on the ground Lisa cradled his strong, lean hand against her face. "I must sing, Mark, and I have a special song now, a message of hope and love. 'Mirror of Brightness' is only the beginning, my way of telling the world the good news of Jesus Christ. Because He died and rose again, human beings can change."

"I know." Mark held Lisa tightly, his lips on the smooth silkiness of her hair. "I want you to sing. I want our life together to be a continual melody of hope. You, Lisa my love, you are *my* song, the song in my heart."

4. Are you interested in buying other Promise Ro-
mances™?

☐Very interested   ☐Somewhat interested
☐Not interested

5. Please indicate your age group.
☐Under 18   ☐25-34
☐18-24   ☐35-49   ☐Over 50

6. Comments or suggestions?

7. Would you like to receive a free copy of the Promise
Romance™ newsletter? If so, please fill in your name
and address.

Name _____

Address _____

City _____ State _____ Zip _____

7370-6

Dear Reader:

I am committed to bringing you the kind of romantic novels you want to read. Please fill out the brief questionnaire below so we will know what you like most in Promise Romances™.

Mail to: Etta Wilson
                Thomas Nelson Publishers
                P.O. Box 141000
                Nashville, Tenn. 37214

1. Why did you buy this Promise Romance™?

☐ Author   ☐ Recommendation
☐ Back cover description   from others
☐ Christian story   ☐ Title
☐ Cover art   ☐ Other_____

2. What did you like best about this book?

☐ Heroine   ☐ Setting
☐ Hero   ☐ Story line
☐ Christian elements   ☐ Secondary characters

3. Where did you buy this book?

☐ Christian bookstore   ☐ General bookstore
☐ Supermarket   ☐ Home subscription
☐ Drugstore   ☐ Other (specify)_____